PODWITCH

PODWITCH

Book I in the **PODWITCH** Sequence

N J Poulton

Matador
9 Priory Business Park,
Wistow Road, Kibworth Beauchamp,
Leicestershire. LE8 0RX
Tel: 0116 279 2299
Email: books@troubador.co.uk
Web: www.troubador.co.uk/matador
Twitter: @matadorbooks

ISBN 978 1800463 165

British Library Cataloguing in Publication Data.
A catalogue record for this book is available from the British Library.

Printed and bound in Great Britain by 4edge Limited
Typeset in 11pt Minion Pro by Troubador Publishing Ltd, Leicester, UK

Matador is an imprint of Troubador Publishing Ltd

For Laura

There are dark shadows on the earth,
but its lights are stronger in the contrast

Charles Dickens
The Pickwick Papers

PROLOGUE

WHITEHALL LONDON
1940

Raindrops tumbled from the night sky, hurling themselves at pavements outside the imposing government building. Soldiers nursing rifles flanked its entrance. Their eyes barely flickered as a car emerged from the darkness and drew to a halt. Its driver slid out and scanned the road in each direction before opening a rear door.

Stepping from the car, the Aldhelm stared up at the building. Thunder rolled overhead as searchlights combed the sky; the German bombers were conspicuous in their absence. She reached for the Pod beneath her overcoat. Its warmth offered relief. Splashing past the soldiers, she pushed through a rotating door. A lantern swung above it in the breeze.

Inside, marble floors stretched beneath giant chandeliers. Men wearing pinstripe suits were gathered in hushed groups at the foot of a broad staircase. As the young woman entered, they turned to look at her. A figure dressed in dark grey broke away and approached.

'Mrs Wainwright?' he asked, extending a hand to the Aldhelm.

'Yes,' she answered, taking it and noting the sweaty, brittle fingers that grasped her own.

'Gretchley's the name. We hoped you would be here sooner.'

His voice was urgent. Mrs Wainwright noticed that his complexion was almost as grey as his suit. A rumble of thunder caused him to glance nervously at the windows.

'Let us waste no more time,' he hissed.

Gretchley wheeled away, making for the stairs. His footsteps sounded insignificant in the building's cavernous hollows. Following him, Mrs Wainwright nodded to the other men. They stared at her, resembling hostile children in an unfamiliar playground.

The staircase turned back on itself three times before joining an oak-panelled landing. It was adorned in coats of arms and stern portraits. Gretchley led her to a door.

'You may enter,' he said.

The Aldhelm hesitated.

'How is he?' she asked.

Sweat glistened on the small man's upper lip.

'Tense…' he replied.

His eyes kept flicking to the window at the end of the corridor. Thunder cracked overhead and he jumped. For a moment, his abrupt manner dropped, revealing uncertainty beneath. But it reappeared instantly. He flashed her a smile.

'You must ensure the prime minister's safety,' he whispered.

'It is my highest priority, Mr Gretchley.'

'Then please, be swift.'

He raised tight white knuckles and rapped on the door. There was a pause.

'Come!' growled a voice.

Gretchley stepped back. He looked pointedly at the handle. Mrs Wainwright took a breath and turned it, pushing against the weight of the door with her shoulder.

Inside, red carpet spread across the floor and bookshelves lined every wall. In front of a sash window stood a desk the size of a rowing boat. Its surface was hidden beneath papers, charts and maps. Opposite was a fireplace, framed beneath a carved wooden mantel. Within it, a fire blazed.

To one side of the hearth was a sofa. On it sat a man, staring at the flames. As the door closed, he leaned on a walking stick and stood, igniting a tiny explosion of dust motes in the firelight. Broad and slightly hunched, he looked part human, part bulldog. A cigar jutted from the corner of his mouth and his eyes beaded with intensity.

'Aldhelm,' he barked. 'It's about time.'

'I'm sorry for the delay, sir. Things are going badly. Labyrinth gateways are failing across the land and the Severals allow me no rest.'

'Bloody annoying,' grunted the prime minister. 'No respect. None at all. They distract you, while the Luftwaffe keeps sending its bombers.' He squinted. 'Where's your Chattan?'

'Whisper is keeping watch over *Podwitch*,' replied Mrs Wainwright.

'Want a drink?'

'No, thank you. It's best we get you on your way. The motor car is waiting.'

The prime minister reached for an overcoat and bowler hat.

'Quite right, quite right. Let's be off then,' he muttered. 'We'll use the back staircase. It exits onto a side street. Gretchley has arranged for the chauffeur to meet us there.'

He stomped to the wall of books and reached for a discreet handle jutting from a shelf. A section of bookcase swung open, revealing a stairwell. The Aldhelm moved towards the opening and stared into it, waiting until she felt warmth from the Pod at her neck.

'It's clear,' she said. 'I'll go first.'

She moved slowly in the gloom. Their footsteps were muffled in the tightness of the small space. The air tasted stale and damp. After several minutes, the prime minister stopped to mop his brow.

'I'm getting too old for this sort of thing,' he grumbled.

With a sudden movement, Mrs Wainwright flung a hand to her chest.

'What is it?' demanded the prime minister.

'The Pod, it's turning cold. Something's wrong. We don't have much time.'

They descended the remaining steps quickly, reaching a cobwebbed passageway that led to a door. Motioning for the prime minister to wait, the Aldhelm approached it cautiously. A heavy key jutted from the lock. She listened but could hear nothing above the sound of heavy rain. The Pod was icy cold against her skin. She pulled it from her coat, bathing the corridor in intense blue light. The prime minister gasped. She waved him forward.

'Stay close to me. Do not linger. Your life may depend on it.'

He nodded, his eyes wide in the Podlight.

Mrs Wainwright opened the door. Rain threw itself at her in a frenzy. But it didn't prevent her seeing the Severals, lurching and crawling in the night. Buildings opposite were thronged with them, and the street itself was a twitching parade of shapes.

'My God,' she said sharply. 'We have been betrayed.'

Holding the Pod up, she let its light flood out of the doorway. The creatures peeled back, keen to avoid its touch.

'I see nothing, Aldhelm,' said the prime minister. Uncertainty hovered at the edge of his voice.

Mrs Wainwright shielded her eyes from the rain and looked for the car. It was parked a little further along the street.

Grabbing the prime minister's arm, she drew him close.

'It's not far,' she cried. 'Do not step outside the light.'

Then they were away, stumbling through the storm. The Podlight carved a path through the assembled throng as the Severals scrambled from it, lifting their heads to sniff the air. Their ranks closed again once the humans had passed and they skulked swiftly behind.

As they neared the car, Mrs Wainwright was relieved to see its engine was running. She raised the Pod, covering the vehicle in protective light, and banged with her fist on the roof. The driver hopped out and opened a rear door.

'You go on ahead, sir,' said the Aldhelm, pushing the prime minister in.

'What about you?'

'I'm staying. There is work to be done here. I'll meet you at Chequers.'

Winston Churchill looked lost. He peered at her from the back of the car. When he spoke, his voice sounded small.

'How bad will things become, Aldhelm?'

'This is the beginning,' she grimaced. 'This is just the beginning.'

She slammed the door. The engine of the Daimler roared into life and it pulled away, leaving her standing, the Pod raised above her head.

Shapes writhed at the edge of the blue light, tightening around it like a fist. Excited snorts emanated from all directions and jagged nails tore at it, but they were unable to penetrate it.

Turning to the building, she saw someone framed in the open doorway, staring at her. It was Gretchley. Severals slithered close by but made no attempt to approach him.

'You?' cried Mrs Wainwright.

Gretchley held her gaze for a moment and then yanked the door violently shut behind him.

Besieged by the hordes of shifting darkness that surrounded her, the Aldhelm tightened her grip on the Pod.

'This is just the beginning,' she repeated.

Another peal of thunder rolled overhead. It sounded like a murmured threat.

LONDON
SOMETIME RECENTLY

ONE

Ravenmaster

———————

The Ceremony of the Keys drew to a close, accompanied by the usual bustle as tourists murmured and nudged each other. Somewhere in the crowd a mobile phone rang.

The Ravenmaster sighed as he pulled up the sleeve of his dress robes and glanced at his watch. Perfect timing as usual, but the evening had dragged and he was in a hurry to get back to the birds. Earlier, they had pecked half-heartedly at some raw beef, eventually turning their backs on it altogether. Even Harvey, the eldest of the ravens, had ruffled his feathers and stood to one side, quiet and morose, not like him at all. They had been unsettled for days now.

George Wardle had been Ravenmaster at the Tower of London for over ten years, nurturing most of the birds since they were chicks. Only Harvey had been there before him. The legend of the ravens was world-famous, and it was a responsibility George had taken very seriously since it had been bestowed upon him.

He glanced up at the damp December sky. Clouds hung heavy above, dimming the night. The recent weather had rendered the grass a dark, scraggy brown, and the stone of the Tower walls seemed to ooze moisture.

'Maybe I should change meat supplier,' George muttered. 'The beef must be bad. That'll be why they're off their food. I'll get some good stuff in. They'll soon be feeling as right as rain.'

'Talking to yourself again, George?' asked another Yeoman as he wandered by. 'Can't you stop worrying about those bloody birds? They can take care of themselves.'

'Night, Bill, you cheeky sod!' retorted George, trying to disguise his concern.

He turned away as visitors were escorted out, making his way through a side door that accessed a corridor running the length of the building.

George had always overseen his duties impeccably, never questioning the daily repetition of his role. Each evening, before the Ceremony of the Keys, he made sure the ravens were in good health, locking each cage door securely and checking them carefully. Normally, when the ceremony was finished, he would change out of his robes and then head straight to his rooms. But tonight, the well-being of the ravens was weighing heavily on his mind. He wanted to see if they'd decided to finish the meat.

Clouds continued to thicken overhead, making it difficult to see. With every step, George found himself wishing he'd brought a torch. The walls stood imposingly over him as he walked the passageway, silent witnesses to a cruel history. Reaching a door, he took a heavy key from his pocket, unlocking it with well-practised ease. He was about to open it but stopped. He lifted his head. The smell of cigarette smoke hung in the air.

'Now where's that coming from?'

George glanced over his shoulder.

'Hello?' he called. 'Anybody there?'

No response, just a cloying silence. He waited, frowning, and then opened the door and stepped through, pulling it shut behind him. He could just make out the silhouette of the ravens' lodgings in the distance and made his way towards them.

Halfway across the square, he could see the metal doors hanging from their hinges, bent and twisted. The wire surrounding the enclosures had been torn from the frames and lay on the ground. George began to run, as fast as his old legs would carry him, his hat flying off, a tightness restricting his throat. He pulled up short and stared. Something was moving inside the cages. Something darker than the night.

'Oi! You there!' George cried. 'What the hell have you done?'

The figure shifted down low to the ground. Its form seemed to stretch in the darkness, indistinct and restless. The hairs on the back of George's neck stood on end and he blinked, just to make sure of what he was seeing.

It sniffed the air, holding its position for a moment. And then it was moving quickly, skulking across the grass. It paused at the wall before slithering up and over the ancient stones.

George stared at where it had disappeared before turning his gaze back to what was left of the birds' lodgings. He hesitated and then made his way to the wall, where a bell hung. He yanked on the rope, sending an alarm clanging loudly between the Tower's walls.

As he did so, a gap in the clouds allowed moonlight to fall across the courtyard. George's hand froze on the bell rope.

Feathers lay scattered across the cage floors. Amongst them lay the bodies of the ravens. The Ravenmaster scanned each of them in turn. He knew them by sight. His eyes landed on a large body lying at the back corner of a cage.

'No,' he whispered. 'Not Harvey too.'

Footsteps pounded across the courtyard behind him, coming in answer to his call.

George knelt, lifting Harvey's body gently. The bird's neck had been broken and feathers had been torn from his body.

'My God,' he whispered. 'Who would do this?'

A hand on his shoulder caused him to look up. The Chief Yeoman was staring at him through wide eyes. There was sweat on his brow.

'The unthinkable has happened, George,' he said. 'The protection has been breached. We must summon the Aldhelm.'

George Wardle nodded as tears filled his eyes. He nestled the body of the ancient raven to his cheek.

T W O

Absence

———————

Cal Wainwright frowned in the darkness, not sure what had woken him at first. A sudden noise? No, it was the absence of something. He couldn't hear his dad's snoring.

'Not again,' he murmured.

His eyes rested briefly on the luminous stars his mum had stuck on the cabin ceiling years before. He paused, double-checking his ears weren't deceiving him before flinging back the duvet. Being on a boat, the door slid rather than swung outwards. Cal opened it slightly and peered through the gap.

Light from the main cabin crept along the corridor towards him. The oil lamps were lit. He slid the door wider and stepped through.

His dad's bedroom door was open. The bed hadn't been slept in. Cal followed the corridor, passing through the galley kitchen. Two saucepans hung from nails in the wall above various odd jars of tea, coffee and sugar on the worktop.

The main cabin was small but cosy. A low table squatted on a faded yellow rug at its centre. A coal-burning stove sat against one wall, the grate glowing with embers. Two chairs were positioned either side. On one of these lay Twilight, Jeb's black and white cat. At Cal's approach, she lifted her head and stared at him. Her eyes seemed to glow in the lamplight.

'Looks like he's gone out again, Twilight,' said Cal. 'That's four out of the last five nights.'

Twilight had been around since Cal was born, which put her at older than fourteen. But her coat was glossy, and she was in good condition. She was tall and moved gracefully. Cal rubbed a hand over her head and down her back.

'What's he up to?'

Twilight purred as he stroked her, arching her back and padding against the cushion. Cal glanced around the room for any clue as to where his dad had gone. He'd been used to Jeb's occasional forays after dark; they'd happened for as long as he could remember. But now it was every night. An image of the little orb that hung around Jeb's neck came to him. He frowned and shook his head, moving to the front doors and pulling them open, letting the chilly December night air sneak into the cabin. Twilight darted through his legs. She stood between him and the gangplank leading to the towpath. Her tail flicked restlessly.

'It's okay, I'm not going anywhere,' Cal said. 'I just wanted to see if Dad's about.'

Steep concrete walls stretched up on either side of the canal, forming a man-made valley through which the water stretched in each direction, meeting a tunnel one way and turning a gentle corner in the other. It was bordered on one side by a towpath. Dingy orange light lay across the concrete, pouring down from the street above. The distant hum of London was the only sound. But there was no sign of Jeb.

As Cal turned back to the cabin, his eyes fell across the picture that hung above the stove. While he'd inherited his dad's blue eyes and square jaw, Cal's sandy hair and slightly upturned nose belonged to the woman in the photo. He always felt a surge of emotion when he looked at her smiling image.

'What do you reckon, Mum?' he said.

Twilight settled on the chair, continuing to watch him.

Outside, the narrowboat sat quietly on Regent's Canal. On its side, in beautiful swirls and colours, was its name.

It was called *Podwitch*.

THREE

Watched

———————

'Your dad's always been a bit weird, Cal. You know that,' said Janey Wickthorpe, staring down at the mobile phone in her hand. Her fingers darted across its screen in a blur. 'Remember he had you believing some of that make-believe stuff when you were younger?'

Janey's short crop of bright orange hair was the only splash of colour against the concrete of the playground. Defeated piles of murky slush slouched in its corners from recent snow showers. A Christmas tree stood outside the main entrance. Blown by the wind, its lights hung forlornly to one side. Groups of kids hovered restlessly, waiting until they could return to the warmth of classrooms.

Cal shifted awkwardly.

'Yeah, I know. But I thought it was just a phase he went through after Mum left.'

'That was years ago. Why would he start again now?'

'I dunno.'

'Well, you should ask him,' said Janey. 'Simple as that.'

'I guess so,' replied Cal uncertainly.

'Remember when he used to go on about river pirates?' said Janey, smiling. 'It was kinda fun back then, looking for them on the canal. But we never really believed it. Did we?'

'Maybe a bit,' said Cal.

'You told me there was a force field around the boat which protected us.'

Cal did his best to smile.

'Just another one of Dad's stories.'

'At least I never believed *that* one.' Janey sent another text and then looked up at him. 'Listen, I'm gonna check out Kate's new mobile. Her dad gave it to her as an early Christmas present. Wanna come?'

'That's okay. It's not like I know anything about them anyway.'

'Yeah, that's another funny thing about your dad. Why won't he let you get one? You're thirteen.'

Cal glanced at the ground.

'Not every kid has a mobile.'

'Yeah, but he doesn't have one either. And you don't even have a normal phone on the boat.'

Jeb's refusal to install electricity on *Podwitch* meant Cal couldn't join in the usual conversations about TV or the internet. But Janey had never seemed to care. It was true she loved her mobile, but she was happiest when outside, spending hours in the park behind her house, climbing trees or swimming at the lido in summer, always proud to display her latest scars. Her eyes had shone at Cal's description of life on a boat when they first met. They'd been friends ever since.

Janey flashed him a grin and then was off. Cal watched her sprint away, her usual white trainers with their laces undone, instead of regulation school shoes. He wanted to tell her the truth but instead had often found himself telling her only parts of it, to make things appear more normal.

He hadn't told her about Jeb's recent nightly excursions, just that he'd been acting oddly. He was too embarrassed to tell her half the things that were strange about his life. She'd think he was nuts. Denying some of the things he saw and heard every day had been hard at first, but now he almost believed he was normal. It was just his dad who was weird. He knew Janey was right; he would have to confront him.

Cal sighed, folding his arms across his chest against the cold. There were just a few more days of term before the Christmas holidays, but he didn't feel the normal excitement. He just wanted things to be normal.

A spiky burst of laughter blasted across the concrete. Cal glanced over to where Jason Pike was wrestling with another boy while the self-appointed school bully, Dean Broad, shouted encouragement from the sidelines. Cal grimaced.

He was about to turn away when a subtle movement on the street caught his eye. A man was watching the playground through the wire fence.

Instinctively, Cal ducked behind the corner of the wall. He waited before peering round. The man wore a long coat, buttoned all the way to the collar, which was pulled up around his neck. His shoes glinted like black mirrors. He had bright blond hair and his face was gaunt and deathly pale. Sunglasses covered his eyes. A cigarette jutted from the corner of his mouth, smoking gently. His hands were buried deep in his coat pockets.

Whether seconds, minutes or hours passed, Cal wasn't sure. He just knew that while the stranger watched the playground, he couldn't help watching the stranger.

The man stood like a statue. The way he stared at the playground was unnerving. Eventually, he let the cigarette drop from his mouth, grinding it under his heel. He turned and moved away, out of sight. Cal waited before leaning back and closing his eyes.

'Bloody hell, Cal, you look like you've run a marathon.'

Cal opened his eyes. Janey was looking at him oddly.

'You're sweating like mad. Did I miss something?'

Cal ran a hand across his brow and was surprised to find his fingers covered in moisture, despite the cold. His chest heaved and he fought for breath.

'Are you okay?' said Janey.

Cal nodded as the bell signalling the end of lunch trilled across the playground. He was grateful for the interruption and bent to pick up his bag. As he made his way to the school building, Cal couldn't help glancing over his shoulder to where the stranger had stood. He could barely stop himself shaking. But it was nothing to do with the cold.

FOUR

Baron

C al reached the canal towpath as raindrops began to hiss across the surface of the water like an angry snake. He'd struggled to keep warm all afternoon and couldn't get the stranger out of his head. As he approached *Podwitch*, he studied the narrowboat that was his home.

Fifty-seven feet long and painted black on the top, with a bright red base, the letters spelling out its name were etched in bright blue and green. Midway along the roof, the stove-pipe chimney smoked furiously in its battle against the elements. Cal was looking forward to the comfort of the cabin and the stove at its heart.

Stepping down into the cabin, Cal noticed the oil lamps were struggling to light the room against the gathering darkness.

'Welcome home.'

Jeb Wainwright spoke without looking up. He was bent over the worktop that divided the kitchen and living room. A dismantled clockwork watch lay in front of him and he was tinkering with it, using a set of small tools. He wore a special set of glasses that magnified his vision of the tiny mechanism.

Cal draped his coat over a chair and dropped his bag on the floor.

'How's work, Dad?' he asked.

Jeb looked up, whipping off the glasses. His blue eyes glinted sharply, despite the cabin's soft light. He looked young for his age, with little evidence of grey amidst his shoulder-length dark brown hair. He was wearing his favourite plaid waistcoat, from which hung an antique gold pocket watch.

'Slow,' he replied. 'People just don't need good old-fashioned watches like they used to. Not with all these newfangled smartphones and digital watches about.'

Jeb earned his living as a watch restorer, the bulk of his work coming from Cooper's Timepieces, a shop in Kentish Town specialising in antique watches and clocks.

'I remember a time when I'd arrive back on *Podwitch* with a bag full of old watches that needed some sort of repair. Every week that was. It's completely different now. This is the first in a month.'

Cal could recall Jeb laying watches out on the kitchen worktop, examining each closely, identifying what was stopping their ancient insides from working. Sometimes he used to let Cal glance through his magnifying glasses at the back of an open watch. Cal had loved looking at the whirring cogs and listening to the tiny tick-tock as they toiled away busily. But that was before Mum had gone.

Things changed after that.

'There's more craft in one of these than anything you can buy today,' Jeb sighed, taking in the dismembered watch.

Cal knew his dad loved his work, and although he didn't earn a fortune, it was enough to fund their simple life.

'How was school?' asked Jeb, putting his glasses back on and leaning forward.

'Usual,' answered Cal.

Part of him wanted to tell his dad about the man he'd seen. But he fought the compulsion and turned away, heading for his cabin.

*

After Jeb had finished work, they cooked sausages and mash together and then ate in silence. Cal jabbed at his food with a fork, but every time he took a mouthful he saw the stranger leering across the playground and could barely swallow it.

'You know I went out last night, don't you?' said Jeb.

Cal froze.

'I found you asleep in the armchair when I got back. I carried you to bed.'

Cal put his fork down slowly and nodded.

'Was that the first time?'

'No, I've heard you going out for the last few nights.'

'You didn't say anything. Don't you mind?'

'That's why I tried waiting up. But I guess I just got tired and fell asleep. What's happening? Where did you go?'

Twilight leapt up onto the back of the armchair behind Jeb. Her eyes were trained on Cal the whole time.

'I had to go to the Tower of London,' said Jeb.

'The Tower of London? In the middle of the night? Why?'

'Listen, Cal. We need to talk. But there are some things I need to check first. You're just going to have to trust me on this.'

Jeb's hand had moved up to the charm that hung around his neck, a round grey sphere, attached to a chain by a small gold loop. He pulled it out from his shirt and rolled it between his fingers, lost in thought for a moment.

It was then that a sudden boom, like a distant explosion, reverberated along the canal, causing *Podwitch* to rock slightly on the water. Jeb leapt to his feet and moved to a porthole. He flicked back the curtain and stared out into the darkness.

'Oh no,' he muttered.

Twilight was on all fours, her back arched, tail flicking. Her fur was standing on end.

'What is it, Dad?' asked Cal.

Jeb reached for his jacket and slipped it on.

'Stay out of sight, Cal. Whatever you do, don't let them see you,' he barked.

'Who?'

Jeb was about to whirl away when he stopped.

'River pirates,' he whispered.

He yanked open the front doors and dashed up the steps. Twilight followed him. Another boom rocked the boat gently. This time, it was louder. Cal swallowed and counted to three before crossing to the porthole and carefully lifting the curtain.

What he saw trapped the breath in his throat.

Emerging into the evening gloom from the concrete tunnel a few hundred yards away was a battered tugboat, filthy and caked with grime. A stout funnel at its centre belched out thick fumes. Another explosion sounded and a mass of smoke rose up, leaving a stain against the orange streetlamp above. What looked like rows of flaming torches burned along each side. As it approached, Cal could make out people on deck; men and women dressed in grubby clothes. Daggers and handguns were shoved into thick leather belts at their waists. They moved quickly, low and sideways in darting runs.

Cal heard the engine cut out. It was stopping. Brash shouting and swearing echoed around the canal, bouncing off the concrete walls that stretched to the streets above. Jeb held the charm at his neck. His lips moved as he said something, then he let it go. To Cal's horror, he began waving at the pirate vessel. It responded by changing its course and turning towards them. As it neared, one of the figures tossed over a rope, which Jeb caught neatly. He knelt and tied it off, securing the boats together.

Cal sensed a movement on the next narrowboat and saw old Mr Bentley peer through the lace curtains in his window. He stared in the direction of the bizarre boat but showed no reaction. Seeing Cal, he waved, before disappearing. He couldn't see them!

Cal flicked the porthole latch and pushed it slightly open.

A group of figures had gathered at the edge of the deck and were staring across at Jeb. They resembled something from a nightmare, all hunched shoulders, tattoos and facial piercings. They appeared human, but their hair was sparse and their skin was sunburnt. As dry as old leather.

'Aldhelm!' one of them bellowed. He held a flaming torch in his hand and his bald head glinted in the firelight. A black patch covered his right eye and he stooped under a heavy-looking hunchback. 'I request permission to come aboard!'

Jeb hesitated.

'There must be no tricks, Baron,' he replied.

Silent tension fizzed as the hunchback stared. He ground his teeth together slowly, causing his jaw to move from side to side. Then he began to move, shuffling awkwardly and pushing others out of his way. He swung himself over the edge of the boat and down onto *Podwitch*, still gripping the flaming torch.

'Dad?' Cal called out, eyeing the large sword that rattled at the pirate's side.

Jeb turned sharply.

'Stay there!' he snapped, thrusting a hand towards Cal. He waited until Cal nodded, then turned away, his fingers clenching and unclenching.

Baron moved with a shuffling limp. Close up, Cal could see a livid scar running from his forehead, beneath his eyepatch and halfway down his cheek. His face was gaunt, his skin weathered. Fully upright, he would stand nearly seven feet tall, but such was the weight of his hunchback, he was forced to bend low. His head was level with Jeb's waist, and he craned his neck back to peer up at him.

Twilight was sitting now, but her eyes did not leave the pirate for a second. A low, threatening whine was coming from her mouth.

Baron held out a hand. Jeb paused before taking it in his own.

'We don't normally see you in these parts, Baron. To what do we owe the pleasure?' asked Jeb.

Baron grinned. His eye glinted.

'I'm a firsty man,' he said, wiping the back of a hand across his mouth. 'Just got back from Paris. It's been a long crossin'.'

'Whisky is all I have.'

'Lovely.'

Jeb moved out of sight. Cal could hear him rifling through the store cupboard outside the front doors. Before he could react, Baron had darted forward and lowered his eye to the porthole in front of Cal, so that it stared directly at him.

'And who 'ave we 'ere?' he whispered, his breath clouding the glass.

'M… m… my name's Cal.'

'Pleased to meet yer, Cal. Baron's the name and piracy is my game.' The big man grinned, his rancid breath forcing its way through the small gap in the porthole. 'So, you're the next Aldhelm, are yer?'

'The what?' Cal frowned.

'Oh, come on, boy. Don't play games when I'm bein' so nice. It's quite a responsibility,' continued Baron. 'To guard the Pod, I mean. Not sumfin' I'd wanna deal wiv.'

'I don't know what you mean,' said Cal.

Baron moved quickly, his hand darting through the open porthole. He gripped Cal's chin, turning his head round so that he was forced to look directly into the river pirate's eye.

'I wonder if you've got what it takes,' Baron hissed.

Cal tried pulling his head back, but Baron's grip was too strong. His fingers were cold and hard. Cal was about to call for Jeb when, for a brief moment, something softened in the pirate's features.

'Well, well. I do declare there's sumfin' of yer muvver in yer,' he said quietly.

'You knew Mum?' said Cal.

Baron nodded slightly.

'Very well indeed. A fine woman,' he whispered. 'Yer dad was a lucky man.'

Cal heard a low whine. Twilight was watching them closely.

'Baron!' called Jeb. 'Here's your whisky.'

'Don't listen to everyfin' they says about us,' said the pirate. 'You and me 'ave more in common than you might fink.'

He gave Cal a last strange look, then winked and turned away, holding out his hand. Jeb gave him a bottle.

'Everything all right?' he asked, flashing a glance at Cal.

'Just lovely,' said Baron, spinning the screw top off the bottle and throwing it into the canal.

He tipped the whisky to his lips and drained it in loud gulps. Half of it ran down his chin. When the bottle was empty, he threw it into the water and belched loudly.

'Not bad,' he said, wiping the back of his hand across his mouth. 'Now, Aldhelm, there's somefin' I'd like to propose to yer.'

He reached up a bristling arm to Jeb's shoulder and drew him away from the porthole, moving towards the front of the boat. Although Cal could hear their voices, he wasn't able to make out anything they said. Twilight was sitting on the deck, staring at him through the porthole.

Cal ducked back inside and followed the muffled thud of footsteps along the corridor to his room. He crept towards the porthole and opened it slightly, peering up at the two men.

'No one has seen him? Are you sure? I mean, absolutely sure?' Jeb asked.

'Well, thass the trouble, ain't it? You can never be one 'undred percent. That is, ahem, unless certain agreements can be made first that might persuade me to be sure.'

There was a pause.

'You know what the killing of the ravens signifies, Baron. You also know what'll happen if the Labyrinth is breached.'

The pirate said nothing.

'What is it you want?' asked Jeb.

'You know what I want, Aldhelm,' said the pirate darkly.

'And you know that's more than I can give,' answered Jeb.

Baron chuckled.

'Well then, I guess you'll know where to find me if you want more information,' he said, 'but I do suggest you fink about it carefully. Remember what's at stake.'

Baron looked fiercely into Jeb's eyes before his face creased into a beaming smile and he roared with laughter. Behind him, the line of pirates on the tugboat burst into raucous guffaws that reverberated around the canal. Baron leaned forward and pulled Jeb into a great bear hug, slapping his back several times before releasing him. He winked as the engine boomed into life and scuttled back across the deck. Despite the weight of his hunchback, he scaled the gap between the boats like an athlete.

Jeb untied the rope as smoke belched up from the funnel and the filthy vessel began moving in the direction of Camden Lock. Shouts and curses filled the air, resonating through the night. As they pulled away, Jeb reached for the orb that hung at his neck, speaking quietly under his breath.

Cal ran through the cabin and up onto the deck.

'Who the hell is that?' he demanded.

'Baron's a river pirate, Cal. I've known him a long time. Since before we came to London.'

'Come on, Dad. Stop kidding around.'

'They rob, cheat and kill, and are generally pretty unpleasant. At the moment, they're with us, but you'd do well to remember never to trust them,' Jeb continued.

'I'm too old for fairy tales, Dad. Who is he really? What did he want?'

'Not now. We'll talk another time.'

Jeb remained where he was, staring nervously at the bizarre boat until it had disappeared from view.

FIVE

A Sinister Approach

'Cal Wainwright,' Miss Hartbury said sharply. 'Listen when I'm talking to you. Do you know the answer or not?'

Cal sat upright and looked at the meaningless numbers on the whiteboard. They had something to do with triangles, but he had found himself drifting off into thoughts of Baron and the stranger at the school fence, and couldn't concentrate.

'Erm, sorry, no, Miss Hartbury,' he said meekly, sending a wave of sniggers throughout the room.

'Quiet!' Miss Hartbury barked at the class. Behind her, Dean Broad and Jason Pike were pulling stupid faces. 'Cal, I don't know what's got into you, I really don't. You can stay in detention over lunch. You and I will discuss

Pythagoras and his theory in some detail, which should ensure today has not been a total waste of time. Meet me in G-2 and don't be late.'

At twelve o'clock, the bell rang and the usual scramble ensued. Dean Broad made a beeline for Cal and bumped into him, spilling his books all over the floor. Smirking, he kicked them across the room and headed through the door. Cal hated to admit it, but while he thought Broad was an idiot, he was clever enough to ensure he was never caught causing trouble by any teachers.

Cal picked up his stuff and jammed it into his bag. When he arrived for detention, he found the classroom empty. He went to the window. Excited cries and the sound of footballs smacking brick walls gently mocked him. Shouting reverberated across the playground and he looked to where Jason Pike and Dean Broad were jostling a year seven kid. Cal grimaced.

'How come I get detention while those idiots get to cause mayhem outside?'

He was about to turn away when he saw the stranger again. Standing in exactly the same place as the day before. He was staring at the children through the fence.

At the same time, a sudden silence enveloped the playground. Although everyone was still playing, Cal could hear nothing.

The man stepped towards the fence, so that he was almost touching it. He called out to a boy nearby. It was Dean Broad. At first, he didn't appear to hear the stranger. But then he turned, and the man nodded to him, smiling.

'Don't do it… don't move,' Cal muttered under his breath.

Dean Broad hovered for a moment then swaggered forward, hands in his pockets. The stranger waited, still smiling. Cal felt tension surge from his shoulders to his fingertips. His heart was pounding.

When Broad reached the fence, the man's smile widened. He bent forward and started saying something. Broad listened, occasionally nodding. Jason Pike had stopped what he was doing. He seemed uncertain whether to join his friend or remain where he was. In the end, he stayed put, watching nervously.

Eventually, the man stood back. An unpleasant sneer spread across his face and he turned and strolled casually down the street. Dean Broad remained where he was. His shoulders seemed more stooped than they had moments before, as though a great weight now rested on them.

Waiting several seconds, Cal allowed himself to take a breath. But then something else caught his attention.

From behind a tree, close to where the stranger had stood, someone, no, some*thing* was moving into the open, its form undefined. It throbbed and shuddered as what looked like two legs seemed to grow beneath it, pushing it up from the ground like an unfurling fungus. Cal blinked, glancing around to see if anyone else had noticed. Dean Broad stayed where he was, staring at the floor. Jason Pike was next to him. Neither seemed to have seen it.

Cal looked back at the thing.

It was taking on a vaguely human shape, although

devoid of specific features. Its surface flickered and shifted as he watched. What resembled eyeholes, roughly in the place a face should be, stared at nothing as it sniffed at the air. It swung its head slowly across the playground, lifting its gaze up the wall of the building until its eyes came to rest on Cal.

Goosebumps ran over his skin like an infection.

The thing sniffed again. Its form shifted more quickly, seeming to enjoy feasting on his scent. Then, very slowly, it moved away, in the same direction as the stranger, out of sight behind the playground wall.

'Glad to see you're on time, Cal,' barked Miss Hartbury as she bustled into the room. 'Now let's see if we can make up for earlier, shall we?'

Cal leaned down to pick up his bag, taking another glimpse from the window as the sounds of the playground returned.

Dean Broad remained where the stranger had left him, staring at the ground.

*

Walking to his next lesson, Cal's mind was racing. He was only just able to pay enough attention to find his classroom. When Janey spotted him, she charged over and slammed her bag down on the desk.

'How was detention?' she demanded.

'Tell you later,' Cal replied.

Last through the door came Dean Broad. He made his way towards Cal, dragging his coat along the floor, moving slowly. His eyes seemed dazed and didn't leave Cal. Jason Pike was following behind, frowning. Broad stopped at Cal's desk and stood over him, his lips moving silently.

'Hi, Dean,' Cal muttered. He didn't know what else to say.

Dean Broad stared at him.

'Hi,' he said after a second.

'Everything all right?'

The whole room had fallen quiet. Everybody was watching. Mr Sutton still hadn't turned up.

'He said to give you a message,' Broad mumbled. He spoke slowly, as if dredging the words from somewhere distant in his mind. The corners of his mouth kept turning down, giving the impression he was fighting a compulsion to say things he didn't want to. 'He told me he hopes the ginger cat makes it and he's looking forward to seeing you later.'

Cal felt Janey tense up beside him and Pike flashed him a frown. When Cal looked back at Dean, he was astounded to see tears flooding down his face and heaving sobs shaking his frame. The whole room was silent.

'Dean, what on earth is the matter?'

Mr Sutton had stopped in the doorway, a look of surprise on his face. Broad didn't respond.

'He's feeling ill,' said Pike quickly. 'Shall I take him to the sickroom?'

'Yes, please, Jason, but hurry. There's a lot to get through today.'

Pike avoided Cal's eye and put an arm on his friend's

shoulder, steering him across the room. Dean Broad's sobs wracked the air all the way along the corridor.

SIX

After School

'What the hell was that all about earlier?' asked Janey, over the sound of scraping chairs. School was finished for the day. Everyone was in the usual rush to get out.

'Forget it,' replied Cal. 'I'll see you Monday.'

He threw his bag over his shoulder and jogged from the room, ignoring Janey's calls. He needed time alone.

Nothing Mr Sutton had said during the lesson had registered. Instead, Dean's words had tumbled around his head like clothes in a tumble dryer:

'He hopes the ginger cat makes it and he's looking forward to seeing you later...'

As Cal passed a window, he saw kids flooding through the playground, spilling onto the pavement. At his locker, he took out his gym bag and slung it over his shoulder.

CRASH!

A fist slammed the locker door shut from behind, causing a metallic bang to echo through the room. Jason Pike glared at him. Another boy stood behind him, looking edgy.

'What did that freak say to Deano?' Pike demanded.

Without Broad, Jason Pike just wasn't as convincing in the bad guy role. Cal could sense fear in the bigger boy. Whatever happened to Broad had really upset him.

'I dunno. I think the message must have been for someone else.' He answered as casually as he could.

'Liar!' shouted Pike. 'You know something and you better start telling me or I'm gonna… I'm gonna…'

'Gonna what?' demanded Cal.

Pike took a step back. He wasn't used to other people standing up to him.

'I don't know what Dean was talking about,' Cal continued. 'What else do you want me to say?'

For a moment, Pike appeared to want to labour the point, but instead he drove his fist into a locker door and stormed out, followed by his accomplice.

Cal closed his eyes. The stand-off was over.

*

Outside, the early evening carried an icy promise. A breeze picked up a pile of litter, hurling it into the air. Cal watched it spiral over the fence. He let the door close behind him and walked across the deserted playground.

Preoccupied, he didn't see Janey on the pavement until he bumped into her.

'Bloody hell, Cal, watch where you're going, will you!'

She rubbed her arm, scowling.

'What are you doing here?' Cal asked. 'I told you I'd see you on Monday.'

He shot a glance left and right along the street. The sky was darkening and the streetlamps fizzed on, bathing them in orange light.

'I saw what happened today,' said Janey, watching him closely.

'Saw what?'

'Dean talking to that bloke. Then I saw him speak to you and then he started crying.'

'So?'

'Is it something to do with your dad acting weird? Does he owe this guy money or something? I just want to know the truth. You know you can talk to me.'

Cal looked at the floor and kicked out at a stone, sending it skidding into the road.

'Suit yourself,' said Janey after a moment. 'Come on, let's go. It's freezing.'

She darted ahead, leap-frogging a bollard and landing awkwardly on her knee. She stopped to examine it before looking back with a beaming smile. Cal grinned at her, glad for her company.

He was about to tell her to wait when silence descended, not the normal hush of a quiet city street, but a void, totally empty of sound. Janey's smile died. Her eyes widened, focusing on something behind him. A look of alarm came over her face and she made a strange squeaking sound. Cal turned and found himself face-to-face with the stranger.

SEVEN

Portent

_____

The man was standing in the middle of the pavement, so that any attempt to pass would have meant brushing against him. His hands were buried deep in the pockets of his coat. Despite the evening gloom, sunglasses still covered his eyes. A mocking grin twitched at the corners of his mouth.

Intense cold ran over Cal's body like a pair of icy hands. Janey had frozen where she was.

'Your friend is fine,' the man whispered. 'She cannot hear us. My words are for you alone, Cal Wainwright.'

It wasn't an ordinary whisper, but one that came from infinite depths, as loud and uncomfortable as a chainsaw. Cal resisted the urge to place his hands over his ears.

The stranger smiled.

'You are entering a world you know nothing about,' he continued. 'It is important you make the right choices.

Do as you're told and you will profit greatly, unlike your father, who has chosen the life of a fool. He has allowed a breach in the Labyrinth and an unstoppable force has begun to ease into London.'

Cal couldn't speak. It was as though something had clutched hold of his throat, letting through just enough air to allow him to breathe.

'I always knew Jeb would struggle. He is altogether too… human. Do not make the same mistakes, Cal. There are significant things happening all around you. You would do well to learn from them.'

The man smiled again, showing a set of perfect white teeth. But the smile hung there only briefly before a low whine, eerie and menacing, sounded across the street. The stranger snarled and spun towards it. Fury was etched on his face. Cal looked across to the source of his rage.

Hundreds of cats of all colours, shapes and sizes covered the parked cars up and down the street. They stared defiantly at the stranger through vivid yellow eyes, their collective moan growing in intensity. It was a haunting sound, like wind blowing across a lonely moor. With every second, more appeared, swelling their numbers.

Cal looked back at Janey. She blinked at him in surprise, no longer paralysed. With the stranger distracted, he pulled her behind a parked car where they crouched, watching the scene unfold.

'What's happening?' Janey whispered.

'I… I'm not sure.'

The stranger had been surrounded and drew his hands from his pockets, bringing with them a pack of cigarettes. He took one and lit it, inhaling the hot smoke and blowing it into the air. It was then that Cal saw his fingernails for the first time.

Where a normal person's would end, short and rounded, the stranger's were sharpened into points and encrusted in grime. Cal's stomach churned just looking at them.

The stranger broke the silence.

'So, the Chattan grow bold,' he grated.

'Chattan?' whispered Cal. 'That's what Dad always calls—'

'Shhh,' said Janey. 'I want to listen.'

A series of hisses and spits came from the cats.

'Oh,' mocked the stranger. 'I forget that you are unable to speak at this hour, and remain very much the dumb animals you are. Well, when your voices return, you can use them to inform the Aldhelm that we are coming. He would be wise to prepare for events the like of which have not been seen on this puny planet for thousands of years. This time, we will not be denied.'

He drew his hands once again from his pockets and brought them together in a clapping motion.

In answer, five shapes appeared from a storm drain next to the kerb. They squeezed up through the grill and stood alongside the stranger, just ten feet from where Cal and Janey crouched. Shifting and throbbing, they lifted their empty eye sockets upwards, inhaling the air about them. One of them groaned and turned towards the children, twitching as it sniffed their scent. The cats bared their teeth and yowled angrily.

'Cal!' hissed Janey. 'What's wrong?'

'Don't you see them?'

'See who?'

'Those… things…'

She stared at him and shook her head.

The cats had sunk low, their tails flailing madly. Cal braced himself, wondering how they could fight things that appeared to be made of shadow.

'Stop!' cried the stranger. 'This is not the time or the place.'

'What do you want then?' shouted Cal, surprising himself.

He swallowed as the stranger turned to where he and Janey crouched.

'So, the future Aldhelm has guts, does he?'

A collective yowl surged up from the cats, causing a momentary flash of fear to appear in the stranger's eyes.

'Before I go, know this,' he rasped. 'There is no way that Podmagic can stand up to the coming of the Mist. Our power has become great since the Guardians locked us away. You would do well to consider the side on which you choose to fight.'

Cal returned a look he hoped was defiant, although underneath he was quivering with fear. The stranger let his cigarette fall to the floor. He ground it into the pavement with his heel before turning, hands once more in his coat pockets, and walked to an alleyway between two houses. Just before he entered it, he stopped and turned back.

'I'll be seeing you again, Wainwright,' he whispered.

A moment later he had gone.

Before there was time for anything else, a distant voice and the sound of running footsteps came closer.

'Cal? CAL!'

'Dad!' Cal cried out, jumping up.

At the sound of Jeb's voice, the throbbing shapes moved faster, snorting for a scent of him. But then they drew together and, moving as one, followed the stranger into the alleyway and out of sight.

Cal turned back to the cats. To his amazement, the street was clear of them. The sounds of distant London had returned, a comforting drone, rendering things normal once more.

'Are you okay, Janey?' he asked.

She looked at him, speechless for a moment.

'Are you kidding?' she exclaimed. 'That was amazing! That weird guy, and all those cats. What the hell is going on?'

'Listen, Janey,' Cal said, his voice urgent. 'Go home, quickly. I don't want Dad to know you were involved in this.'

'Why?'

'He'll only get all funny on us. Make out it's something it's not.'

Janey regarded him cynically from beneath her short crop of ginger hair.

'What are you talking about? It *was* weird. I can help tell him about it.'

'Janey, please. Look, I'll talk to him. I'll let you know what he says tomorrow. Okay?'

Janey's eyes frowned disapproval. She pursed her lips.

'Okay,' she said. 'You'd better.'

Janey turned and retreated into the gloom, kicking out at a twig angrily. Cal heard Jeb's footsteps approaching. He turned to greet him.

'Hi, Dad,' he said, doing his best to smile. 'What are you doing here?'

Jeb had been running and was breathing heavily.

'Are you okay?'

'I'm fine, Dad. What's wrong?'

Jeb looked relieved. His eyes combed the street. 'You sure you're okay?'

'Really, I'm fine. Why?'

Jeb's chest heaved. He brushed a hand through his hair.

'It's just… something's happened… something bad.'

'What do you mean, Dad? What's happened?'

Jeb paused and put his hands on his hips.

'Nothing,' he said, forcing a smile. He ruffled Cal's hair. 'I didn't want to miss you, that's all. Sorry for being melodramatic. Come on, let's get out of the open.'

Jeb put his arm protectively around Cal's shoulder, guiding him along the street. His grip was firm.

*

After they had gone, cars passed by and Christmas lights flashed in windows. On one side of the street, a cat lay on the roof of a car. It stared intently through half-closed eyes, watching the entrance to the alleyway where, not long before, the pale stranger and his group of shifting shadows had last been seen.

EIGHT

Night Visitor

—————

C al lay restless in bed. He'd avoided Jeb's awkward questions by saying he had homework to do and wanted an early night. But every time he closed his eyes, he saw the stranger's cruel smile.

Dean Broad's reaction had been shocking, but after his own direct contact with the man, Cal could understand why.

'I just want things to be normal,' he whispered. 'Living on a boat without electricity is bad enough, but this is getting crazy.'

He heard Jeb make his way to his own cabin. Maybe he wasn't going out tonight.

A dim orange glow from the streetlamp permeated the porthole curtain. Cal found its familiarity reassuring. He turned to the stars on his ceiling and waited. Should he tell his dad about the sinister stranger and his message?

He kicked his feet in frustration under the duvet. He was sick of having to think about it. He just wanted to sleep.

A short, sharp rattle sounded at the porthole. Cal sat upright.

'What the hell was that?' he whispered.

The same clattering sound splintered the silence again. He swallowed, listening for any sign that Jeb had been disturbed. Hearing nothing, he knelt on his bed and raised a hand to the porthole curtain. Very slowly, he drew it across, peering out into the gloom.

It was a minute or so before his eyes adjusted and he saw someone standing on the towpath, concealed by shadows. Whoever it was, was waving to him.

'Janey!'

Janey stepped into the light. Cal signalled to her to stay where she was before jumping out of bed and pulling on his clothes.

Another shower of small stones cracked sharply against the porthole. He had to move fast. She would wake Jeb at this rate. He finished dressing and inched quietly from the room.

The oil lamps in the main cabin had been turned low and coal glowed in the stove. There was no sign of Twilight. The coast was clear. Cal slid back the bolts on the front doors, wincing as they scraped slightly. He eased one door open and squeezed through the gap.

Icy moisture had begun to freeze to a silvery sheen on *Podwitch*'s roof. A wisp of smoke trickled up from the chimney, looking like a lazy genie. Cal closed the door behind him and crossed the walkway to the towpath.

Janey was loitering in the shadows further along.

'You took your time,' said Janey as he approached. 'I thought I was gonna have to smash that window to wake you up.'

'It's nearly ten o'clock. What are you doing here?' asked Cal. 'Do your parents know you're out?'

'Don't be daft. I managed to sneak out. Dad's away on business and Mum got an early night. She had a headache or something. So I thought I'd come down and see what your dad said about that freak. Cool, huh?'

She flashed him a cheeky grin.

'I told you I'd talk to you on Monday.'

'That's ages away. Come on, Cal. I want to know what's going on. Did you speak to your dad or what?'

Cal looked away, wishing he had Janey's appetite for adventure.

'Come on, Cal. You did tell him about the freak and the cats, didn't you?'

Cal stayed silent.

'What's wrong with you?' asked Janey.

'Nothing, leave it.'

'You know something and you're not telling me. That's it, isn't it?'

'I said leave it,' Cal snapped.

'What is it, Cal? What's going on? I'm your mate, aren't I?'

Cal shifted awkwardly.

'Yeah, of course you are.'

'So come on. Are river pirates planning to rob some ships?'

Janey's laughter echoed loudly off the surrounding concrete.

'Shhh! I told you to leave it, Janey. I knew you'd take the mickey. I'm going back to bed. You can get lost.'

He began marching back to the boat. It was then that the smell reached him. Bitter and sweet. Cal stopped and stared into the deep pockets of shadow lining the towpath.

'What's up?' Janey whispered. She wasn't laughing now.

'Cigarette smoke. Can you smell it?'

Janey lifted her nose and sniffed.

'Bloody hell! You don't think it's him, do you?'

She moved closer and they stood side by side staring into the darkness.

'See anything?' Janey whispered.

'No.'

A breeze came from their left, carrying another cloud of cigarette smoke. Cal turned sharply as Janey grabbed his elbow. He stared in the direction it came from, where the bridge loomed over the towpath.

He thought he saw a tiny orange glow appear in the void of shadow. The orange dot hovered in the air before fading away. Moments later, the smell of smoke came to him again. There *was* someone. Watching them.

Cal stepped backwards. Janey moved with him. Neither of them spoke. Cal was about to turn and lead them back to *Podwitch* when a hand landed heavily on each of their shoulders.

'Well, well,' said a voice. 'What a surprise.'

'Dad!' cried Cal.

'Bloody hell, Mr Wainwright!' said Janey.

Jeb stared down at them, Twilight on his shoulder, her eyes like mini torches in the gloom.

'You really should watch your language, Janey,' he said. 'Everything okay?'

Janey nodded at him, open-mouthed.

'Don't you think it's a bit late to be out and about?'

'I… err… just needed to ask Cal about some homework,' she said, a little too quickly.

'Is that true?' asked Jeb, turning to Cal.

Cal hesitated, knowing his dad wouldn't fall for Janey's excuse. Besides, there was still the question of who, or what, was standing under the bridge.

'I think we should tell him,' said Janey.

'Tell me what?' asked Jeb.

Janey's voice piped up before Cal could utter a word.

'There was a stranger outside school. And loads of cats. Cal said there were some other things. I don't know what.'

'Stranger?' asked Jeb.

'He had claws,' said Janey.

Jeb swallowed. He put his hands on their shoulders.

'Are you sure you're both okay?' he asked, his eyes flicking between them. 'Did he hurt you?'

Cal and Janey shook their heads.

'He just talked, that's all,' said Cal.

'More like whispered,' Janey corrected him.

Jeb watched them closely before rubbing his hands together.

'I think we'd best be getting indoors, don't you?'

he said, following Cal's gaze to the shadows under the bridge. 'There are lots of things we need to talk about.'

'Brilliant!' said Janey, beaming.

At a subtle brush of Jeb's hand, Twilight leapt down from his shoulder and sat watching the towpath as they made their way on board.

NINE

The Aldhelm

Jeb stocked up the stove, piling it high with coal to ward off the night's chill. They settled down, each cupping a mug of hot chocolate in their hands. Twilight arrived shortly afterwards, pushing through the front doors and settling on Jeb's lap.

Janey was bubbling with energy and Cal sat back, allowing her to give her version of events.

'Janey, did the stranger know your name?' Jeb asked when she had finished.

'No.'

'Your address? Anything like that? Think carefully, it's important.'

'No, nothing. He hardly noticed me at all. He only spoke to Cal.'

'Good. Well, that's something at least.'

Jeb stood and leaned on the kitchen worktop.

Twilight dropped silently to the floor.

'The whole thing was set up,' he continued. 'I only realised when the Pod gave me warning.'

'Pod?' asked Janey.

Cal shot her a look. It looked like his dad was going to start getting odd.

'What happened?' asked Cal.

'I delivered the watch I've been working on to the shop and was going to come back to *Podwitch*, but Mr Cooper told me he had an emergency, an urgent repair for a new customer, willing to pay above the odds.' Jeb scratched his head, recalling the details. 'I didn't think about it at the time, but Mr Cooper told me it'd be worth my while and that he'd split the cash with me. Things haven't exactly been busy recently, and with Christmas around the corner I had to take it. So I stayed and did the work.'

He slammed a fist down onto the worktop.

'How could I have been so damn stupid?' he said. 'I should have known better. To risk leaving you, even for five minutes, was the stupidest thing I could have done.'

'It's okay, Dad,' Cal said.

'No, Cal, it's not okay. I exposed you to something extremely dangerous and that was unforgivable. It's thanks to the Chattan that you're both safe.'

Cal glanced at Janey.

'You mean the cats?' he said. 'That's what you used to call them when I was younger, wasn't it?'

'That's right,' said Jeb, 'but they're not ordinary cats by any means.'

'I remember that too. You used to tell me Twilight could speak,' Cal said, shaking his head. 'And to think I believed you.'

An awkward silence hovered between them for a moment.

'There were loads of them there, Mr Wainwright,' said Janey, keen to fill the silence. 'I've never seen that many cats in one place in my whole life. And the weirdo seemed pretty scared of them.'

Jeb pulled his gaze from Cal and looked at her, smiling gently.

'The Nephilim have a dislike for large numbers of Chattan. They find them somewhat intimidating. But there's not much that scares you, is there, Janey?'

'Not likely, Mr Wainwright. I can hack it, whatever it is. They say a problem shared is a problem halved or something like that. Well, I reckon that's true.'

'Okay,' said Jeb, his voice firm. 'It's important that you know what's happening. Cal, it involves you directly, whether you like it or not. Janey, after this evening, you are implicated too. Once you have come to the attention of the Nephilim, they will not forget you.'

'The what?'

'Nephilim. The main adversaries of the Pod Guardians.'

'Here we go on the crazy train again,' mumbled Cal.

He looked across to Janey and was surprised to see her face rapt with attention.

'How am I involved?' she asked.

'Thorne saw you with Cal tonight. That was enough.'

'Thorne?'

'The Nephilim.'

'I can't believe you're gonna bring all the old stuff back up, Dad,' interrupted Cal. 'It sounds mad!'

'Mad or not, you can't go on ignoring things happening all around you,' said Jeb gently. 'Surely it must be dawning on you that there's some truth in what I've been saying all these years. Think of the pirate's visit yesterday, and the Chattan you saw this evening. Think about Thorne. You have to admit it's not exactly normal.'

'He's got a point, Cal. There's some pretty strange stuff going on,' said Janey.

Coals shifted in the stove, followed by a pop and a shower of sparks.

'I think now's the time to find out how bad things are, if you're both interested?' persisted Jeb.

'Wicked!' said Janey.

Cal said nothing.

Jeb pulled the little orb from around his neck and held it up. 'This is a Pod,' he said. 'It's one of many all round the world. They were created before time – as we know it – existed, and contain power beyond imagining,' continued Jeb. 'They can show you the past although they cannot take you there. They will defend you and warn you against danger. They help to protect the world from those who would upset the delicate balance.'

'You see, Janey?' said Cal, interrupting. 'It's completely crazy. I've had to grow up with this. It got worse when Mum went.'

Pain was briefly etched across Jeb's face. Cal fell quiet;

he had gone too far. But he was sick of the fairy tales.

'Enough, Dad. I just want it to end,' he continued, more calmly. 'I want you to be normal. I want the internet, a mobile, electricity for God's sake. Instead, we live on a damp old boat, with oil lamps. It was fun once, but I'm tired of it.'

'We can't have any of those things on *Podwitch*, Cal. It's unthinkable.' Jeb shook his head.

'Why?'

'Pod Guardians can never use mobile phones for communication. The Nephilim are tapped into the wires that carry voices, electricity supplies, even broadband, to houses across the land. Which is why we use our trusted allies, the Chattan, to pass messages over great distances, sometimes from country to country.'

'You mean the cats?' asked Janey.

'Yes, the cats,' said Jeb.

'But come on, Mr Wainwright. Are you trying to tell us that your Pod-whatsits use cats to send messages instead of phones or email? That's ridiculous. It must take ages. What if you wanted to get a message to someone abroad?'

'It's a good question, Janey. I'm afraid the world of the Pod Guardians is mired a little in the past. Technology has advanced rapidly in the last century, a little too rapidly, so much so that it's too easily corrupted by those seeking to do harm. We have to stick to simpler methods. Believe it or not, the Chattan network is faster than you might think, with messengers covering short distances and passing on details to the next, and then the next, and so on. They're not just cats after all. They have evolved alongside the Pod Guardians over the centuries.'

'That's enough!' said Cal, standing. 'Janey, you should get going. You don't have to listen to any more.'

'Wait, Cal,' said Janey. 'Maybe there's something to it…'

Cal stared at her.

'It's kinda fun, even if you don't believe it.'

'You should go home,' he said, whirling away, heading towards the front doors.

'Stop, Cal. You can't go out there alone. It's not safe anymore.'

Jeb's voice was quiet. He sounded tired.

'The Nephilim know who you are. That means the Severals will be looking for you. And for Janey…'

Cal stopped, his foot on the first step.

'I know you've seen them,' continued Jeb. 'It's because things are changing. That's what I've been trying to tell you, why I've been going out at night. You leave *Podwitch*'s protection and they'll find you. Whether tonight, tomorrow, or next week. They'll find you.'

Twilight shifted on the armchair, pushing herself up into a sitting position.

'You must know I'm right. Besides, I need your help.'

Cal stared at the little wooden doors. He had protected Janey from this for so long and now it was spilling out of control. He wished he could disappear, be anywhere else but here.

'Cal?'

He felt Janey's hand on his elbow.

'We saw some strange stuff today. Let's give your dad a chance at least.'

Cal sighed. He turned back to the cabin.

'You need my help?' he said.

Jeb nodded, saying nothing.

'What do you mean?'

Jeb looked down at his hands.

'I think it's time, old girl,' he said, glancing across to Twilight.

'Time for what?' asked Cal.

'Time I showed you proof.'

'Proof of what?'

'That I am the Aldhelm,' said Jeb.

There was that word again.

'The… what?' retorted Cal.

'The Aldhelm,' Jeb repeated. 'It's an old English word meaning protector or guardian. You see, I am the Guardian of the Pod, and you will be its protector after me. *You* will inherit it.' He leaned forward, eyes narrowing. 'And it's the most important job in the world.'

TEN

The Podmap

J aney was staring at Jeb in awe.

'Janey?' Cal said. 'Oh, come on, don't tell me you believe it.'

'There's perhaps one thing that'll persuade my own son that I'm not a raving lunatic,' said Jeb, standing up.

'What's that?' asked Janey.

'Evidence,' he answered. 'It's time I showed you just what the Pod is capable of. There's something I need to do, and with what you've told me, the sooner the better.'

Jeb was striding the length of the boat to his cabin. Cal could hear the sound of drawers slamming and things being thrown about.

'Janey!' he hissed. 'What's with you?'

She turned to him and shrugged.

'Snap out of it. I used to fall for this when I was younger but come on!'

Jeb reappeared with something in his hand.

'Right!' he said loudly. 'There's not a moment to lose! Clear the table.'

He held up a folded document, its edges curled and the paper yellowed with age.

'What's that?' asked Cal.

'It's the ticket to your first journey into another world. This piece of paper will open doors that most people think are closed forever.' Jeb's eyes were wide. 'You'd better draw the curtains over the portholes. I'll lock the doors. We can't be too careful.'

Moments later, with the windows covered, the front doors locked and an extra helping of coal on the fire, Jeb unfurled the paper and spread it over the table. Its edges hung over the sides and brushed the floor. Cal could see what looked like faint streets or roads etched across it. Scattered randomly amongst these were lots of blue dots. They seemed newer and more defined, but the ink of whatever old pen or quill had drawn the roads was barely visible. He could make out the odd letter and some shapes that looked like buildings, but little else. Despite his frustration, he couldn't help but feel interested.

'Do you see what it is?' Jeb asked.

'It's a map, I think, but it's not very clear, and I'm not sure what those funny blue dots are either.' Cal pointed to one and looked at his dad.

'Come on, Mr Wainwright! What is it?' asked Janey.

'What I tell you now, you have to swear you will keep to yourselves at all costs.' Jeb's excitement was tinged with seriousness. 'The world of Podmagic is full of amazing things, but it's dangerous too, and as the future Aldhelm, you must remember much of what you are taught if you are to succeed.'

Cal said nothing as Jeb gestured to the yellowed parchment spread before them. 'You're looking at a map of London. It's ancient, as you can see by the colour and condition of the paper. But the most amazing thing about this map is that, despite its age, it is one hundred percent up to date with every road name and building in the city.'

'That makes no sense,' said Cal. 'How can it be up to date if it's so old?'

Jeb smiled mischievously.

'Turn down the lamp.'

Janey jumped up and dimmed the oil lamp, reducing the cabin to near darkness. The orange glow of the streetlamps outside gently probed the curtains.

'Now,' came Jeb's voice, quiet and reassuring. 'Watch carefully.'

Cal was suddenly aware of a blue light, subtle at first but getting brighter. It was coming from the Pod, which was dangling from Jeb's fingers. He was holding it level with his head over the map. Soon the cabin was bathed in a cool blue glow.

'Now take a look at the Podmap,' said Jeb. 'And tell me what you see.'

Cal looked down and gasped.

Where there had been nothing but yellowed parchment and faint outlines, he now saw an incredibly detailed map, drawn in the most beautiful black ink and filling the paper. It was unlike any map he'd ever seen. At the top, in delicate calligraphy, were the words: *The City of London.*

'Do you see it?' whispered Jeb.

Cal nodded silently.

'It's amazing,' whispered Janey. 'I can see London, as though I was a bird looking down. No, not a bird, a pilot or an astronaut! How come we can see it so clearly now?'

'Think of it as a map drawn in a kind of invisible ink, and the Podlight an ultraviolet light that reveals it. But this map will only work with this Pod, never any other, and never an ordinary UV light.'

They watched as a mass of something crossed over the city, obscuring it from view.

'Clouds!' Janey exclaimed. 'I can see clouds moving.'

Beautifully etched clouds floated lazily across the ink-drawn city, disappearing slowly off the opposite edge of the paper.

'Now for the really amazing part,' whispered Jeb. 'You can sit back for this bit.'

Janey had leaned so close to the map that her nose was almost touching it. She sat back.

'Ready?'

Jeb lowered the Pod over the centre of the map. As he did so, the image of the London streets became magnified, their perspective changing as though they were passing out of the sky itself, down towards the city centre. Jeb stopped lowering the Pod and London stopped coming closer; he raised it higher and the ink lines became smaller again.

'It's like an interactive map on the net,' said Janey. 'Where you can zoom right in to see what you want. But I don't get it. There's no computer here and no satellite. And this one's moving, even though it's just an old map.'

'Put it closer again,' urged Cal.

Jeb lowered it and they passed through a clump of clouds at an alarming speed. Jeb held his hand steady and they stopped, suspended above London.

'I can see the London Eye!' Cal exclaimed. He could just make out the gigantic wheel, revolving slowly.

'And there's Big Ben!' said Janey, pointing.

'Okay, we're going to go a little closer now,' said Jeb. 'There's something I need to find out.'

'Find out?' asked Cal.

Jeb lowered the Pod until Cal could read the street names written in old-fashioned, spidery ink. He watched as cars moved along roads and people scurried along pavements like ants.

'Wow!' he whispered.

The Pod began moving in a circular motion, as though his dad was rotating his fist in small circles. But Jeb's hand was still – the Pod was swinging on its own. As it moved, the streets below it moved too, following its motion. It started to swing more erratically, flying in all directions, causing the streets and houses to whirl about faster and faster until, just as steadily as it had started, the Pod began to slow, and the images slowed with it. Roads and buildings passed with less speed until finally, everything was still once more.

Directly beneath the Pod was one of the blue specks, larger now. As Cal watched, a beam of blue light connected it to the Pod.

'What does the plaque say?' whispered Jeb.

'The what?'

'The blue circle on the map, what does it say?'

Cal leaned forward and read out loud.

'Charles Dickens, 1812-1870. Novelist. Lived Here.'

'Dickens, eh?' said Jeb, smiling to himself. 'It's been a while since I've seen him.'

'Seen him?' said Janey.

'Yes, it would seem he has some information for me. He has ten blue plaque properties throughout London, so let's see which one we have to visit. Grab me something to write on, could you?'

Cal stood up slowly, his head swimming. He rummaged through one of the kitchen drawers, pulling out a pen and pad as his dad leaned over the map.

'Right, it's 48 Doughty Street, WC1.'

Jeb scribbled down the address before putting the Pod back around his neck. It was now dull and grey. He stood and turned up the oil lamp.

'It's almost eleven,' he said, glancing at the kitchen clock. 'We can only access a plaque in the hours of darkness, between midnight and dawn. We'll have to get Janey home first.'

'Oh, come on, Mr Wainwright,' cried Janey. 'You can't send me home now, not after that.'

'Yes, I can,' said Jeb firmly. His face softened. 'Look, why don't you see if you can come to *Podwitch* tomorrow?

We'll know more then. You can stay over if you want to. But this time get your mum's permission. I don't want you getting into trouble.'

'What do you mean, access a plaque, Dad? Where are we going?' asked Cal.

'48 Doughty Street, of course,' Jeb replied, pulling a hardback book from the shelf. 'We're going to see Charles Dickens for some information.'

He opened the book, glancing inside before passing it to Cal.

'He gave me this last time I visited him.'

Cal looked at the cover of the leather-bound volume and read its title, handsomely printed in gold leaf: *The Pickwick Papers*.

Inside the cover were a few handwritten lines:

Jeb,
I thought the following line from one of my stories
was most appropriate:
"We need never be ashamed of our tears."
Your good friend,
Charles Dickens

'What does it mean?' asked Cal.

The smile on Jeb's face faltered.

'It wasn't long after your mum left. I wasn't at my best. He pressed this book into my hands without a word. I only read his inscription when I got home. Second only to the Pod, it's my most treasured possession.'

He finished speaking and a brief sadness hung in the air.

'Come on, Janey,' he continued more brightly. 'Let's get you home.'

'What about Thorne and the Severals?' Janey replied. 'Shouldn't we just stay on *Podwitch* if it's protected?'

'The Pod will warn me if they're anywhere near, and protect us if necessary. Now come on, no more stalling.'

Janey shot Cal a sulky look.

'See you tomorrow,' he said.

She didn't reply but stomped up the steps, followed by Jeb.

Cal looked back at the book and considered what Jeb had said. A sense of awkwardness had always surrounded his mum's disappearance and they had hardly ever spoken about it. Cal remembered when she hadn't returned home and Jeb going out of his mind with worry. After days without news, he had left Cal next door with Mr Bentley. The afternoon had turned to dusk and then into night before a knock had come at the door. Cal, who had been dozing under a blanket, woke up as Mr Bentley answered it. It was Jeb. He had been drinking.

'Go and sleep it off, Jeb, and come back for the boy in the morning,' Mr Bentley had urged.

Jeb had tried to argue, but his voice had broken. Cal could see the two men through the front doors of the boat, Mr Bentley with a consoling hand on Jeb's shoulder as he wept. Shortly afterwards, Jeb had left and Cal fell into an uneasy sleep.

The next morning, Jeb picked him up, his face pale and his eyes red. They had walked to Regent's Park where, beneath falling autumn leaves, Cal learned that his mother would not be returning. Jeb hadn't elaborated but it wasn't important to Cal at the time. He'd been too bewildered to cry then, even though Jeb had encouraged him to.

And so those few terrible days passed, and they moved on, never speaking of it again. It seemed better that way, Cal often told himself, although his mum's absence had opened a void in his life that had never been filled.

A coal shifted in the stove, pulling him from his thoughts. Feeling drowsy, Cal shifted in his chair, attempting to keep alert, but soon he drifted into a fitful doze.

ELEVEN

Walking The Streets

———————

'Cal!' Jeb's voice came from far away. 'It's nearly one o'clock. Time to go.'

Cal opened his eyes and sat up. It was dark.

'How are you feeling, sleepyhead?'

'Fine, just needed a little rest.'

Twilight sat in front of the stove, watching as they pulled on their coats.

'Grab your scarf. It's cold out there,' said Jeb, buttoning his jacket.

Twilight stood and stretched. Cal leaned forward and scratched at the back of her neck.

'It's okay, I've decided he should know,' said Jeb.

'What?' said Cal, looking up at his dad.

'Can you please not be so rough, Cal? You've always been a little too heavy-handed,' said a silky voice.

Cal jumped backwards, knocking the table over.

'What the…!' he exclaimed.

'I didn't ask you to stop, just be more gentle,' she said.

Cal gaped. The voice had definitely come from Twilight's mouth; he had seen it move as the words came out. She sat and watched him coolly.

He turned to Jeb, who was watching with amusement.

'I told you to believe, Cal.'

'Are you seriously telling me that she's talking?'

'It's rude to speak about someone when they're in the same room, Cal,' said Twilight. 'And I have a name, as you well know.'

Cal collapsed back into his chair.

'I must be going mad!'

'The Chattan are a very special line of cats that go back centuries, especially bred for the Pod Guardians,' said Jeb. 'We know little about them other than their origins are in Egypt. They appear as normal cats, but in reality are so much more. Each Pod Guardian in each country has a dedicated Chattan companion throughout their life. Without them, we would be lost. Your grandmother gave me Twilight when she was a kitten, twenty years ago. She has been with me ever since.'

'But how can she be talking? And how come I've never heard her before?'

'The Chattan are only able to speak between the hours of midnight and one o'clock, the result of a curse placed on their race long ago. So there really has been little opportunity in life so far for you to hear her. I also made it a rule that on the rare occasions when you were up and awake during those times, Twilight was not to speak, until the day I confirmed to her that she could. Today's the day.'

'And how exactly do the Chattan help?' Cal asked, unable to take his eyes off Twilight.

She answered this question herself, looking icily at Cal as she spoke.

'There are countless numbers of us acting as messengers, carrying information around the world. We hear things that might go unheard and see where people can never go. We are companions to our masters and will fight to the death to protect those we serve.'

Her voice was full of pride and a little arrogance. She watched him for a moment and then began licking a paw.

Jeb leaned across and whispered low in Cal's ear. 'She's really very fond of you,' he said with a wink. 'Now come on, we have to get going.'

Twilight followed them from the cabin, leaping up onto the roof and winding against a flowerpot.

'Take care out there, Cal,' she said. 'I still think it's a mistake for your father to involve you at your age.'

'Pipe down, Twilight,' said Jeb. 'We'll be fine.'

The Chattan turned to him.

'It's not you I'm worried about, Jeb,' she said.

Cal watched their exchange with his jaw open.

'It's okay, Cal,' urged Jeb. 'You can talk to her. She's still the old Twilight you've known all your life.'

'That's easy for you to say.'

Cal stared at the cat.

'It's okay… err… Twilight…' he said uncertainly, moving to stroke her. But he held back. It was all too weird. 'We'll be back soon,' he said quickly, and darted across the walkway.

Jeb led them along the towpath, climbing the concrete steps to the main road. They doubled back, crossing the bridge above the canal into Regent's Park. Cal was uneasy at leaving the streetlamps behind.

'It's one of the unwritten laws that the Pod affords some protection within the parks of London,' Jeb explained.

'But I thought crime happens in parks after dark?' said Cal, looking about warily.

'It does, and I wouldn't travel here without the Pod, Cal. But with it, we will find refuge from the Mist.'

They reached the southern end of the park and emerged in the street, passing beneath Euston Road, heading west. After crossing Tottenham Court Road towards Russell Square, they rested for a few minutes to catch their breath. Sirens echoed in the distance, mingling with the muted rumble of traffic that Cal found reassuring.

'Okay, Cal?' asked Jeb.

'Fine,' he replied.

He'd lost track of their position several times, and only got his reference from Centre Point tower, which appeared every now and again, stretching above the buildings that lined the streets. They had attracted some questioning glances from passers-by, but he could tell that his dad had made many trips like this before, by the way he weaved confidently through the quieter backstreets.

They set off again, and it wasn't long before Jeb

nudged Cal, pointing to the road name written high up on the corner of a building: Doughty Street. They had arrived.

Tall, terraced townhouses stood proud, their arched front doors painted in various colours. High rectangular windows revealed three levels to each house, with two at ground level, alongside the front door, and three on each of the two upper floors. The wrought iron railings fronting each house glinted in the glow from the streetlamps. Behind these, steps dropped down to lower levels and cellars. Few of the buildings were single houses, most having been converted into flats and offices, given away by multiple doorbells and letterboxes at their entrance doors. Jeb and Cal's footsteps echoed on the concrete.

Jeb stopped, looking back the way they had come.

'What's wrong, Dad?'

Jeb hesitated and then put an arm around Cal's shoulder, encouraging him forward.

'Nothing, I just thought… it's fine,' he said. 'Come on, we're almost there.'

Number 48 had a shiny green door and white window frames that gleamed in the lamplight. The iron guttering looked brand new. Cal's eyes picked out a sign on the front wall. It simply said: *The Dickens House.*

'It's a museum now,' explained Jeb. 'You can see the opening times listed below. But look up there.'

Higher up the wall, nestled in the bricks below the middle window, was a blue plaque. Cal recognised it as one of many he'd seen all over London, indicating landmarks and houses of famous people throughout history. White lettering on the blue circle explained who had lived there and when, as well as what they were famous for.

'I thought they were just a tourist gimmick,' he said.

'You thought wrong,' said Jeb.

'*Charles Dickens, 1812-1870. Novelist. Lived Here,*' read Cal. 'Exactly like the one on the map.'

'That's because it *is* the one on the Podmap.'

A distant church bell struck two o'clock.

Jeb glanced up and down the pavement, ensuring that no one was approaching, and moved to the front step of Number 48, pulling out the Pod and lifting it over his head. Cal stayed in the shadow of the tree, unsure what to expect.

A sudden sound caused him to glance along the street.

'Dad!' he hissed. 'Someone's coming!'

Jeb raised a hand in acknowledgement but remained where he was. Cal looked back to where a young couple were walking towards them. From their unsteady movements, he could tell they were drunk. They stopped and kissed.

'Come on,' called Jeb, beckoning to him.

Cal ran forward, grabbing his dad's outstretched hand. Only then did he see that the Pod had begun to glow.

Its deep blue light was spreading quickly along the pavement and up the face of the building, brushing aside the orange light from the streetlamp. The blue plaque was shining too, and a beam of light materialised, connecting Pod and plaque. Cal watched, spellbound, as it grew in intensity. A thundering noise, like a waterfall, began roaring in his ears. As the light increased, so did the sound.

He began to worry that the whole street would be woken by what was fast becoming a deafening crescendo and wondered what on earth the drunken couple would make of the strange scene. He glanced to where he thought they would be standing, but saw that they had gone. In fact, the entire street had disappeared. There was nothing to either side of them, or above and below, but deep blue. It was like standing in a cloudless sky, although he could still feel the firm concrete under his feet. Ahead of them, Number 48 remained clear and solid. Cal gripped his dad's hand tightly and Jeb squeezed back, saying nothing. Keeping his eyes fixed firmly on the front door of the house, Cal shut out the other sensations around him as best he could.

The roaring snapped to a sudden silence, as though a switch had been thrown, and the blue void surrounding them evaporated. Cal found himself back on the pavement. He looked up at his dad, wondering what had happened. Jeb put the chain over his head, tucking the Pod into his jacket.

The couple were just a few feet from them now, laughing together. Cal tried to get out of their way, but Jeb didn't, and the two of them ended up stretched awkwardly across the pavement, still holding hands. The couple kept walking, apparently so drunk they hadn't even noticed them. Cal squeezed his eyes shut, ready for a collision.

But none came.

Instead, he heard the girl giggle, a shrill sound that seemed to come from further along the pavement in the other direction, as if they had already passed by. He opened his eyes and saw that the couple *had* continued in the direction they had been walking, as if he and Jeb didn't exist.

'Did they go around us?' he asked, confused.

'No, Cal, they went through us. You see, the Pod has carried us to a place that exists outside the ordinary progress of time.'

'But everything looks the same.'

'Well, yes, we're not outside physical space, just time. Things are as we left them seconds ago. We are there but not there, just one step removed. Both you and I and the house we are about to enter are outside time and the trappings of physical reality, as is the person we have come to meet,' said Jeb.

Cal noticed that the busy drone of London had fallen silent. All he could hear were the echoes of the couple's shoes as they staggered away.

'How long can we be here?' he asked.

'When you're outside time, all measurement of it can be stopped, or altered to pass as quickly or slowly as necessary. We can be here for a thousand years, or just five minutes.'

Jeb tugged Cal by the hand gently and he moved forward, looking up and down the street that was there, but not there. At the top of the steps, Jeb reached out to the large door knocker.

'Can I do it?' asked Cal.

'Of course.'

He reached up with both hands and lifted the knocker, bringing it down once. A dull thud vibrated through the door. He paused and then did it again. They waited, listening as the sound of footsteps approached, followed by the click and scrape of latches being pulled. Finally, a key turned in the lock and the door swung slowly open.

The man who answered the door was of medium height and wore a short dressing gown over grey trousers and black shoes. He had a bushy black beard and dark hair that sprouted wildly above a high forehead and was swept to one side. A cigarette burned in his hand, and light danced in his eyes.

'Greetings, Aldhelm,' he said in a low voice. 'It's good to see you again.'

It was a voice that carried a strong London twang behind its educated tone.

'Greetings, Mr Dickens,' said Jeb.

'And this is?' asked Charles Dickens, glancing at Cal.

'My son, Cal. I hope you don't mind.'

'Mind? Of course I don't mind. Delighted, young man, delighted.'

He held out his hand and Cal took it, half expecting to meet nothing but cold air. But it was a hand, warm and firm, nothing like a ghost at all.

'Come in, come in,' said Charles Dickens, standing aside to let them through.

Cal and Jeb stepped over the threshold and the door was closed behind them, shutting out the street that was no longer a street at all.

TWELVE

A Growing Danger

Dickens led them through the entrance hall, its floor an elaborate pattern of black and white tiles. Lamps with real flames flickering behind etched glass gave off a low light that reminded Cal of the oil lamps on *Podwitch*. Sepia photographs lined the walls. The hallway opened up, a corridor leading away to a door on the left, and to the right, a flight of stairs ascended to the first floor. They climbed them in silence. A large, ornate glass light hung from the ceiling on the landing, which turned back on itself towards the front of the building.

'We'll use the drawing room this evening,' said Mr Dickens.

They took the second door on the right and entered a high-ceilinged room. A coal fire burned lazy and low in the grate. Next to the hearth stood a wingback armchair and above the mantel hung a large mirror, framed in thick gold. Two sofas faced each other across the centre of the room and in one corner was a small table. A number of paintings were suspended from a rail that passed around the top of the walls, which were a soft creamy colour and had an uneven surface. The floor was of wide wooden boards over which a vast woven rug added a splash of colour. Four gas lamps hissed from the walls, giving off a low light. The smell in the room reminded Cal of old books.

'Please sit,' said Mr Dickens, lowering himself into the chair by the fire.

He threw the remains of his cigarette into the grate and picked up a pipe from the arm of the chair, filling it with tobacco from a leather pouch. Cal and Jeb sat on one of the sofas. Mr Dickens watched Cal's face with wry amusement.

'I am assuming, Master Wainwright, that this is your first journey via the blue plaques of London.'

Cal nodded.

'You will soon learn that many things exist in this life to which you have so far remained completely oblivious. You must embrace them, for it is a journey of wonder upon which you are embarking, one not without its perils, but miraculous nonetheless.'

As he spoke, his eyes held Cal spellbound. They were dark in colour and yet still danced with the light that he had glimpsed at the front door.

'Are… are… you alive or dead?' he asked.

Mr Dickens let out a bark of laughter followed by an amiable chuckle.

'I might well ask the same of you,' he replied.

'But it's the twenty-first century and you're supposed to have died over a hundred years ago.'

The novelist smiled and lit his pipe, puffing gently until it began to smoke.

'True, but consider what your father told you outside. The three of us are meeting in a place unrestricted by the passing of time, where the issue of being alive or dead is of no consequence. We simply, *are*.'

'But how?'

'Well, Podmagic has many powers, and the Pod has passed through the hands of Aldhelm for countless centuries. During that time, they have entrusted a select few as their associates, those who have, shall we say, attained a level of achievement and wisdom that distinguished them within their own lifetime. We, in turn, act as advisors, drawing on our experiences to advise the Aldhelm when needed. I am one of the fortunate ones allowed into the inner circle.'

'So, you were never the Aldhelm then?' asked Cal.

'Alas, no. What I would have given to wield its power. In my day, the Aldhelm made himself known to me after one of my public readings. He was fond of my work and needed help influencing some of the, let us say, higher social circles. I, through my writings, was both an inspiration to him and a practical route to ensure he was able to succeed, and we became firm friends and allies. Imagine my surprise as I was introduced to the same world into which you have stepped so very recently. I understand how you feel, even though I had the benefit of being a grown man when I learned of the world of Pods.'

The novelist took a long puff on his pipe, sending thick smoke drifting above his head.

'And now, gentlemen, let us talk of recent events and why the Podmap has brought you to me.'

'It started two weeks ago, when the ravens at the Tower of London were killed,' said Jeb.

Dickens' eyes clouded, but he said nothing.

'When the Chief Yeoman contacted me,' Jeb continued, 'I knew it could only mean one thing. That the Nephilim had returned. Of course, I began nightly inspections of Labyrinth gateways throughout London, but so far I have found none that have been breached.'

'That, at least, is something,' said Dickens.

'But the Severals have been seen. And my own Nephilim approached Cal here directly. He confirmed that the Mist is on the rise, Mr Dickens, yet I have seen no further evidence of it.'

Dickens watched him carefully, frowning as he listened. He waited for a moment before responding.

'If the Severals have been seen, it means that the Labyrinth has indeed been breached, and the fact that Thorne has been sighted is evidence of that.'

'There is something else,' said Jeb. 'I received a message from an unlikely source just days ago, which is why I'm here.'

'Unlikely source?' Mr Dickens leaned forward, intrigued.

'It was from Baron.'

'That old cut-throat? Do you trust him?'

'I never trust river pirates. But he likes me. We go back a long way.'

Cal wondered what he meant.

'Indeed,' said Dickens, his eyes flicking to Cal. 'Now tell me, what *was* the message?'

'Baron told me that the Baudouin is missing.'

'Baudouin?' interrupted Cal.

'The French Pod Guardian,' said Jeb, glancing at him. 'He has not been seen on the streets of Paris for days. That's all Baron would tell me. I couldn't get anything more from him.'

Mr Dickens sat back slowly in his chair. He made a bridge with his fingers and lifted them to his chin.

'Are you happy for the boy to know all?' he said.

Jeb nodded. 'He's part of it now,' he replied.

'Very well,' said Dickens, removing the pipe from his mouth and laying it on the arm of the chair. 'Your news is grave indeed, Aldhelm, and foretells the coming of your first true test. The sightings of the Severals and Thorne indicate that the Mist may be rising. But the Baudouin's disappearance is the more immediate problem. It leaves a gap in the global network and means Paris is unprotected.'

'You have heard nothing of him through the French plaque network?' asked Jeb.

Dickens shook his head.

'Has this happened before?'

'From time to time, it is necessary for a Guardian to go into hiding, but it is unusual. Worse still, there have been occasions when some have sought to use the Pods for their own ends.'

'Are you suggesting Monsieur Legard could have betrayed us?' asked Jeb.

'It is simply a possibility, Aldhelm. We must rule nothing out. Besides, the Nephilim could not have breached the Labyrinth alone. A Pod Guardian could be a deadly ally if persuaded to assist them.'

Jeb sat back in his chair. 'What should I do?'

'You must attempt contact with Legard through the Chattan network. If they find him, arrange to meet with him in order to determine the nature of what is happening. By contacting you through young Cal here, Thorne has drawn your attention to the growing danger. We must be thankful for that at least, although his motivations remain unclear. You must be vigilant, Aldhelm. Is *Podwitch* well protected?'

'Yes,' replied Jeb. 'We're safe there.'

Dickens nodded.

'Use the book, Jeb. Let it guide you. And trust the pirate only as far as you have to. If the Mist is forming, then those susceptible to wrongdoing are most likely to be influenced by it. You must avoid travel at night whenever possible, and if necessary, walk the Labyrinth. The Pod can guide you through it.'

Mr Dickens stood and faced the fire, his back to them, one hand resting on the mantel shelf.

'So,' he said, 'it comes again.'

His voice carried a chill. Coals shifted in the grate, interrupting the silence.

'When did the Mist last come?' asked Cal.

Dickens sighed and turned to Cal, his eyes sombre.

'The Mist forming is a rare phenomenon, a surge of evil formed by the hands of the Nephilim. These surges are what the network of the Pods guards against. The last significant uprising came between 1939 and 1945.'

Cal wracked his brains; the dates sounded familiar.

'The Second World War?' he asked, unsure.

'Indeed. The Mist grew strong throughout the world then, tearing through nations and driving them mad. It turned rational, normal people into monsters capable of unspeakable acts. But it was unable to fully form, although it came close.'

'You mean, things now could be worse than the Second World War?' asked Cal.

Mr Dickens' eyes became fierce.

'Oh yes, Master Wainwright, much worse.'

Cal barely had time to let this sink in before Jeb was on his feet and moving to the window.

'The Pod,' he barked, his hand reaching for it. 'It's cold. Something's wrong.'

Dickens and Cal followed, cautiously.

'Something's out there,' said Jeb. His voice was clipped and urgent.

'Get back!' he hissed.

He darted to the left of the window, pulling Cal with him. Jeb waited before peering around the window frame.

'What do you see?' whispered Dickens.

'Severals. Opposite the house.'

The novelist shut his eyes and muttered something under his breath. Leaning around Jeb, Cal looked through the window.

At first, he couldn't see anything unusual, but then his eyes were drawn to a movement across the road. Five shapes, dark and impenetrable, were standing beneath a tree. At first, they blended with the shadow thrown by the branches, but their restless movement gave them away. Cal could see how much darker than normal shadow they were. One moment, they were squat and low; the next, they stretched taller, their forms never static.

'Can they see us?' he whispered.

'No,' said Jeb. 'The Severals can't see or hear. They hunt by smell alone. It's rare for them to be so bold. They shouldn't be here. This is the non-time. Have you ever heard of such a thing, Mr Dickens?'

'Never,' replied the novelist. 'I cannot explain it. But things must be worse even than you feared.'

'What happens if they find us?' asked Cal.

'It's one thing for them to be in the void outside time, but gaining entry to Number 48 would be unthinkable,' replied Jeb. 'We must trust the protection. Our biggest problem now is getting away without being discovered.'

He turned back into the room, his face lined with worry. Cal continued watching the five shifting patches of darkness under the tree.

'There is a way, Aldhelm,' said Mr Dickens.

'Tell me,' said Jeb.

'I have a painting, here in this room, a landscape by Constable, a fellow member of the Blue Plaque Network.

You should be able to use the Pod to travel to that very spot from here.'

'It's not Essex or Suffolk, is it?' asked Jeb. 'I don't want us turning up in a field in the middle of the night, eighty miles from London.'

'Hampstead Heath,' replied Dickens. His eyes blazed in the gloom.

'Perfect!' said Jeb.

Dickens led Cal and Jeb to a medium-sized painting of a country scene.

'It faces west, looking towards Harrow. That should be your position when you arrive. I will ensure you are returned at the very minute that you opened the connection with Number 48. Now go on, the sooner you are off, the better.'

'Aren't you coming?' asked Cal.

'I cannot leave the place outside time, Master Wainwright. But I am sure the Aldhelm is right. The protection on my old house will hold firm. Besides, I have ten residences in this great city and can move between them as I wish. Those Severals will still be waiting when I am long gone. Do not fear.'

'Thank you,' said Jeb, holding out his hand. Dickens shook it.

'Hold strong, Aldhelm. We are with you.'

Jeb nodded, pulling the Pod from his jacket, spilling blue light into the room. Charles Dickens looked at Cal.

'Goodbye to you, Master Wainwright. Travel safely, and do not leave your father's side.'

The light danced in his eyes as he spoke.

'Goodbye.'

Cal took Jeb's outstretched hand. He focused on the wide-open space, grass and trees in the painting. The light flared brighter still, and he knew if he took his eyes from the picture he would see that they were once again suspended in nothing but blue. The roaring sound returned, louder than before. He felt himself and Jeb begin to move forward, floating in the air, and as the scene in the painting came closer, Cal could see it changing.

The trees and grass were growing, slowly at first, stretching into larger versions of themselves. The landscape altered as more trees and bushes appeared. Others disappeared. The sky grew dark, turning from daylight into dusk. The glimmer of city lights appeared through the foliage, alien at first but soon familiar. Cal felt a cool breeze on his face, and the smell of old books changed to one of damp earth. Light swelled and he shut his eyes against its brightness, gasping as the roar deafened him. Pressure squeezed the air from his body as though a thousand unseen hands were crushing him. Just as he was about to give into panic, everything stopped.

Cal opened his eyes and found himself looking at a line of trees. He was standing on grass. The hum of city life droned in the distance.

'Are you okay?' asked Jeb.

'I think so,' said Cal, 'although that felt really weird, horrible, in fact.'

'It was a first for me too,' said Jeb. 'I'm not sure I'd like to repeat it.'

'I'd rather that than meet those Severals, Dad!' said Cal, relieved at their escape.

Jeb ruffled his son's hair.

'Well said,' he chuckled. 'Now come on. We need to get back to *Podwitch* and get you into bed.' He flipped open his pocket watch. 'It's two o'clock in the morning.'

So Mr Dickens had been right. They had returned at the exact minute at which they had left normal time.

They turned away from the clearing and had barely walked five paces when Jeb stopped and grabbed Cal's shoulder. His other hand reached for the Pod.

'What's wrong?' asked Cal.

'The Pod, it's cold,' said Jeb, pulling Cal closer to him.

The clearing was still and dark.

'Can you see anything, Dad?'

'No. But the Pod's warming up again. Perhaps it was reacting to our shift through the painting.' Although his words were comforting, he continued to stare at the surrounding darkness as though he himself didn't believe them. 'Come on, let's get going.'

Only too happy at the prospect of leaving the shadowy clearing behind, Cal followed without a backward glance.

*

A little afterwards, the clearing sat hushed and still before what looked like a large stone pulled itself free from a mound of earth and unfurled steadily upwards.

Just visible in the starlight, the Several sniffed the breeze, shifting restlessly. Catching a scent of the Aldhelm and his son, it gave a moan of pleasure before moving in the direction they had gone.

THIRTEEN

From Bad To Worse

The following morning, Jeb picked Janey up and escorted her safely back to *Podwitch*. The weather was cold and crisp so that pavements sparkled underfoot. Cal filled her in on the details from the previous night as Jeb prepared lunch. It could easily have been an amazing dream, but as Cal spoke, it felt as though he was confirming to himself that everything had actually happened. As the afternoon passed, the sky dimmed to a slate grey, and once again a dingy gloom closed around the canal.

'Tell me again,' Janey asked, her eyes wide in the lamplight, 'why I can't see the Severals.'

'Just be happy you can't,' answered Cal.

'But I wanna help, and surely it's better to know when they're around?'

'Janey's right, Cal,' said Jeb, taking a sip of coffee.

'Severals are invisible to those who aren't aware of them, relying on stealth to inflict their damage. The fact the Severals were in the place outside time means they are becoming more powerful. I have no idea how they got there, but it's most likely they followed us somehow. My biggest worry is that they'll have picked up your scents yesterday and can track you easily. We must be cautious.'

'How do I get to see them?' asked Janey.

'Well,' said Jeb slowly, 'the simplest way is to touch a Pod at the same time as its Guardian.'

'Is that the reason I can see them and Janey can't?' asked Cal. 'Because I've handled the Pod in the past?'

Jeb nodded. 'Partly, but more importantly because Podmagic is in your blood.' He looked back at Janey. 'Being given the sight is not to be taken lightly. It means you will have a responsibility to the Pod to do all you can to protect it, no matter how dangerous. You must be brave.'

Janey shot a glance at Cal.

'I can handle it, Mr Wainwright,' she said defiantly.

Jeb smiled.

'Okay,' he said. 'Let's get it over with.'

He took the Pod from around his neck and held it in his palm. Within seconds, the blue glow began to appear at its centre. Janey's eyes widened as she looked at it.

'Bloody hell!' she whispered.

Cal felt hairs on the back of his neck stand up as he saw it again. When the light became too bright to look at any longer, Jeb held his palm out towards Janey.

'You can touch it now,' he said gently. 'Don't let go before I tell you to or the Podmagic will fail.'

Janey hesitated.

'It won't hurt you,' he said. 'It's quite harmless.'

She reached out slowly. As her fingers made contact with the Pod, she let out a small gasp.

'It's warm!'

Jeb said nothing, although his lips were moving silently. After thirty seconds, the light dimmed.

'Are you all right?' Jeb asked, watching her carefully.

'All right?' she beamed. 'That was bloody brilliant! It felt amazing, like the best I've ever felt. Even better than that day I climbed right to the top of the giant oak in the park at the back of mine and could see the whole of London. Remember, Cal?'

Cal nodded, smiling at his friend.

'So now I'll be able to see the Severals?' she asked, jumping up and crossing to a porthole, pulling back the curtain to peer outside.

'Yes,' said Jeb. 'For the rest of your life.'

Janey turned her head left and right, craning to catch sight of something sinister. She turned back with a look of disappointment on her face.

'What if we see that weirdo again?' she asked.

'Thorne? We were lucky the Chattan intercepted him yesterday,' said Jeb. 'But if he approaches you a second time it could be more dangerous. From now on, outside *Podwitch*, you must travel only under protection of the Pod.'

'How's that gonna work?'

'You'll have to stay at home unless you are with me.'

'But it's nearly the Christmas holidays. What about Mum? She'll want to know why. I never stay indoors if I can help it.'

'Tell her you're not feeling well,' Jeb replied. 'I wish it could be different, Janey. But until I can fix things, there's no choice.'

'Okay,' she nodded.

'What exactly are the Nephilim, Dad?' asked Cal.

Jeb paused before answering.

'There have been various definitions of them throughout the centuries, some based in mythology, some based in religion. In fact, they're referenced in the Bible. None, however, outside the world of the Pods, know their true identity and purpose.'

'Which is what?' whispered Janey.

'They are creatures who walk the earth in human form, although they are anything but. They work as agents of the Mist, to pave the way for its coming and to do its bidding in a physical sense. They carry its word, poisoning the minds of those they come across, and commanding the Severals as their foot soldiers. The Nephilim are fearless, and will stop at nothing to achieve their goal.'

'How many are there?' Cal asked. 'Nephilim, I mean.'

'For every Pod Guardian, there is a Nephilim, an opposite, working against them. Neither can exist without the other. It may be that for years they're dormant, lying low until it is time for them to rise once more. It can be centuries between the appearances of the Nephilim, and an Aldhelm can go through life without ever meeting or knowing their opponent. For the Baudouin of France, there is an opposite, for the Bergr of Norway too, and all the other nations of the world.'

As Jeb spoke, he drifted into a trance, his eyes lost amongst the flames in the stove.

'Is Thorne your opposite?' asked Cal quietly.

Jeb sighed. 'Yes, Thorne is the one by which I know him, although he has many names, depending on what he is doing and who he is addressing. You must stay clear of him at all costs.'

'Mr Thorne?' repeated Janey.

'Just Thorne,' Jeb corrected her. 'Listen to me carefully, Janey, this is a very serious business. It's vital you remain indoors until I say it's okay to do otherwise.'

'I already promised, didn't I? Anyway, are you sure I can't go out at all?'

'Not without agreeing it with me,' replied Jeb. 'It's safer in daylight and Thorne or his Severals will be unlikely to approach you if you're with an adult, at first anyway. They rely on intimidation and aim to isolate their targets, especially children, so never travel alone. I just don't want you to take any chances.'

Cal knew how difficult this would be for Janey. She would hate being caged up like a zoo animal.

'What about Dean Broad?' he asked.

'There's not much we can do for him at the moment,' answered Jeb. 'After direct contact, Thorne will know his name, his address and everything about his family. It's out of our control now. Do me a favour though, and report back anything you hear about him, strange behaviour, that kind of thing.'

'I can do that,' said Janey eagerly. 'I only live two streets from him. Mum knows his parents, so I can keep an eye on him that way. I'll see if she mentions anything and I won't have to go outside for that either.'

'Perfect,' said Jeb. He glanced at the clock. 'Listen, it's late. We should all think about getting some slee—'

A sudden sound interrupted him, low and small outside. The three of them froze. It came again, a scrabbling sound, irregular but insistent. Jeb raised a finger to his lips and stood up. Twilight dropped to the floor and crept forward. Cal moved behind the armchair, keen to put something between him and whatever was outside. Janey followed him.

The scrabbling fell quiet. Jeb slowly held out the Pod towards the doors, waiting, hardly breathing. Moments passed before the noise began again. It was more erratic now, as though whatever made it could barely touch the wood at all.

As it continued, the Pod began to glow. Cal heard Janey gasp somewhere to his left.

Jeb stepped forward, holding the Pod in front of him. He glanced at where Twilight crouched ready to spring and slid the bolts back on the doors. Whatever was out there had only to push at them and they would open freely. Jeb hesitated before pulling one open, then the other.

At first, it seemed as if there was nothing there. Jeb inched forward, trying to see if whatever had made the noise had made a run for it. But there was nothing moving along the towpath. He was about to turn back when a strange sound came from somewhere low in front of him.

Jeb looked down and there, lying on the doormat, was a ginger tomcat. He knelt, tucking the Pod inside his shirt. Even in the darkness, the blood on the cat's fur was visible.

'Close the door, Cal,' Jeb whispered, gently gathering the animal up and ducking into the cabin. 'And get me some warm water. Hurry!'

Cal did as he was asked, while Janey stared in horror. Twilight paced restlessly, twirling and jumping up on her hind legs to glance at the cat, which lay limp on Jeb's lap.

The ginger cat was so still, that at first Cal couldn't tell whether it was alive or dead. Jeb whispered soothing words as he dipped the cloth in water and dabbed lightly at the matted fur, attempting to clean the blood away. Whenever he touched the cat, it whimpered, causing Twilight's tail to twitch in distress. Soon the cloth was stained red with blood.

'My God,' muttered Jeb.

Three open wounds ran the length of the cat's body, angry and livid. Even now, fresh blood seeped out of them. One of the cat's ears was missing and a large gash was open under one eye. All over its body, patches of fur had been ripped out.

'Twilight,' Jeb said gently. She didn't seem to hear him. 'Twilight,' he repeated, more firmly. She stopped and looked up. 'Do you know him?'

Twilight made a low moaning sound.

'And is he Chattan?' continued Jeb.

Twilight mewed quietly, rocking from side to side.

'What did she say, Dad?' Cal asked.

'She said yes,' Jeb answered quietly.

FOURTEEN

The Worst In People

'We need to get you away from here, Janey. *Podwitch* may no longer be the safest place in London, and I won't endanger you by keeping you here. We should leave soon. Cal, you'll have to come too. I don't want anyone left alone. We'll make sure the Chattan is comfortable. I'll need to wait until midnight to speak with him. Let's hope he makes it that long. Get me something to keep him warm. Quickly.'

Jeb didn't look up as he spoke.

Cal ran to his dad's room and grabbed a woollen blanket from a drawer. They laid the Chattan gently onto it and placed a small bowl of water close by.

'Are you sure we should leave him?' asked Janey.

'We have to. There's no time to lose,' Jeb answered sharply.

He stepped onto the towpath before waving Janey forward. Cal came last, closing the doors behind him. The Aldhelm gripped the Pod underneath his coat while Cal and Janey stayed close to him, each holding on to his jacket as instructed.

'Keep your eyes forward,' whispered Jeb. 'They won't attempt to approach us while we have the Pod.'

Cal obeyed but after they had climbed the canal steps, he became sure that something was moving on the opposite side of the road, just out of his line of vision.

A group of Severals were clambering across the face of a block of flats, twenty feet above the ground. Below, no fewer than ten skulked along the pavement. Two were crawling over parked cars, sniffing the air.

'Dad?' said Cal, panic in his voice.

'Don't look at them, Cal. Keep walking.'

Jeb increased his pace, which meant the children had to jog to keep up. Janey remained silent, staring straight ahead. Cal noted how tightly she gripped his dad's jacket. The Podmagic had worked; he knew she could see the Severals as clearly as him.

'Which way is quickest, Janey?' asked Jeb.

'Third turning on the right and second on the left,' she replied.

They arrived at a pedestrian crossing.

'Keep looking down,' said Jeb, his voice tight.

The Severals were hovering on the pavement opposite. As cars flew by, Cal could sense more of them arriving.

The beeps sounded and Jeb was off, crossing the road. As he neared the kerb, he pulled the Pod over the neck of his jacket. It shone brightly against his chest.

A gasp eased from the assembled Severals, like a gust of wind blowing through the branches of a dead tree. They parted, creating an opening just wide enough to ensure the Podlight didn't touch them. Jeb drew the children close as they stepped into the throng of darkness.

The Severals shifted menacingly and Cal could hear them sniffing as the Podlight continued forcing them apart.

Within seconds, anger had welled up from deep within him; at the loss of his mother, at the fact his dad was risking their lives and at Janey for forcing her way into his big secret. He looked across at her, overwhelmed by a fierce desire to lash out, to send her running away from him and his dad forever.

They hadn't got far when a crash of metal sounded behind them, followed by the terrible silence that descends seconds after a road accident. A man's voice echoed across the street.

'Are you all right? I'm so sorry, I don't know what happened.'

Cal and the others turned in surprise as the Severals began moving away from them, heading to where two men were climbing from their cars.

The bonnet of one was crumpled and steam poured from beneath it, while the boot of the other had a huge dent, and its bumper hung twisted and broken. The drivers were speaking calmly, one gesturing at the cars, the other standing with his arms folded, nodding. Their exchange was good-natured, and they appeared mainly concerned with each other's well-being.

The Severals surged towards them, their pursuit of the Aldhelm forgotten. They formed a large circle around the scene of the accident. Completely oblivious to the throbbing shapes surrounding them, the two men continued talking. But as Cal watched, a change came over them and within seconds the conversation had turned aggressive, with lots of finger-pointing and raised voices. More Severals scrambled to get close as the scene unfolded, the sky crackling with their excitement as the men became more agitated.

'What's happening?' whispered Janey.

'The Severals are drawing the worst from them,' replied Jeb. 'It's like a sport to them.'

Other people were stopping to watch as the row became more heated. The circle of shapes pushed closer, buoyed by the mounting tension. The men, who'd forgotten about the accident itself, were concentrated now on goading one another. The throbbing and shifting of the Severals became more frenzied. When the first punch was thrown, Jeb turned the children away.

'Come on, we must go while they are distracted.'

The sounds of fighting and angry shouts came from behind them. Cal turned for a last glimpse but could see nothing of the two men. They were buried beneath a mass of writhing shadow.

Cal considered his feelings for Janey when he had been near the Severals. He had felt nothing but animosity and the desire to strike out at her. Had the same thing started happening to him too?

Jeb led them on, flicking regular glances over his shoulder. They turned into the next street, finally arriving at Janey's house, a redbrick semi that had seen better days.

'Remember, Janey,' said Jeb, 'don't leave the house without informing either Cal or me. I'll arrange for a Chattan to keep an eye on the street. If you need to communicate with us, use the cat.'

'Gotcha,' said Janey.

'Now, in order for me to place a protection on the house, I'll need an object from inside.'

'Okay, what's best?'

'Something that never leaves the building. Think quickly, Janey, the Severals won't be long.'

'I've got it!' she said, running up the steps to the front door.

Cal and Jeb waited with their backs to the house, watching for any sign of movement along the street. After a minute or so, the front door opened behind them. Janey was holding something in her hand.

'It's Mum's favourite ornament. It's been on the windowsill for as long as I can remember. I know it doesn't look like much, but I guess that doesn't matter, does it?'

It was a porcelain figure of a dog, ten centimetres high and dark brown in colour.

'No, that's fine,' said Jeb, flashing her a quick smile.

He held the Pod against the ornament. Light spilled out as he closed his eyes, muttering under his breath.

After ten seconds or so, Jeb pulled the Pod away, handing the figure back to Janey.

'Go inside now and get some rest. We'll pick you up in the morning before school. Remember what I said. Not a word.'

'Yes, Mr Wainwright,' replied Janey, nodding. She turned to Cal. 'See you tomorrow.'

She ran back up the steps, stopping halfway and swivelling round to face them.

'How will I know which cat will be the messenger?'

'You just will,' said Jeb. 'Now off you go.'

Janey waved and disappeared inside.

'We'll take a different route back,' said Jeb. 'I'm almost tempted to use the Labyrinth, but no, things aren't that bad yet.'

*

Back on *Podwitch*, the wait until midnight was almost unbearable. The injured Chattan lay quietly, eyes closed, seeming to drift in and out of consciousness. More than once, Jeb held the Pod close to the animal, letting soft blue light drift over him. Each time, it seemed to bring him some relief. Twilight lay curled in one corner, her eyes not leaving them.

At midnight, Jeb reached out a hand and gently laid it on the Chattan's side. The ginger tom stirred and opened its eyes. Jeb leaned over him carefully.

'A m... m... message,' the cat rasped. 'From... Le... Legard.'

'Steady now,' said Jeb. 'You know something of the Baudouin? Where is he?'

The cat swallowed, its tongue lolling unnervingly from its mouth.

'He… will… c… come,' it gasped.

'When? When will he come?' asked Jeb, stroking behind the cat's ear.

'Be… fore… the passing… of two moons… on… the Heath… Parliament… Hi… Hill… You… m… must watch for the… mist.'

An unpleasant gurgle came from its throat and it shuddered.

'Well done,' said Jeb. 'Now rest.'

For a moment, the Chattan's eyes closed, and he breathed shallow gulps of air. But then a shudder ran across his body. His limbs twitched uncontrollably before finally falling still.

'Dad?'

'It's too late,' Jeb said quietly. 'He's gone.'

As Cal watched, colour started draining from the cat, and its form steadily became more and more faint until it was hard to make anything out at all. Soon there was nothing left, just spots of blood on the blanket.

As Twilight yowled mournfully, Cal turned away, his eyes growing hot with tears.

*

'Was it Thorne?' asked Cal.

'Without question,' replied Jeb.

He had washed and changed and was leaning up against the kitchen worktop, his arms folded. The porthole curtains were drawn, and the stove was busy fighting the December chill that was threatening to engulf *Podwitch*.

'Direct attacks on the Chattan are incredibly rare. Thank God he got to us before he passed away,' he continued. 'At least now I know Legard is alive, and that he's coming here.'

'Where did the Chattan's body go, Dad?' asked Cal.

'Somewhere he can rest. When someone, or something, dies fighting for the Pod on protected ground, like *Podwitch*, they are taken to a place where no more harm can be done to them.'

Twilight was curled in front of the stove, inconsolable.

'It will be hard on her to see one of her own kind dying like that. She won't have seen it before,' added Jeb.

Cal crouched and stroked her. The fact she was able to speak had quite gone from his mind. She was just the same old pet he'd always known, in need of comfort.

'It's starting, isn't it, Dad? The badness,' replied Cal.

'Yes, it is, and we're at the tip of something that may last a long time. What happened tonight changes things.'

'You think Thorne meant to kill the cat? Not just hurt him as a kind of threat?'

'Those wounds were intended to take life, no doubt about it.'

They sat in silence for a few minutes before Twilight stood and moved to Cal, purring as she climbed onto his lap.

'See,' said Jeb. 'I told you she liked you. Now come on, we need to get some sleep.'

Cal smiled, encouraged that Twilight had sought him out for comfort. He rested his hand on her fur, knowing that ahead of them lay an uncertain road.

*

Across the city stood the home of Dean Broad. Similar to Janey's semi-detached house, it stood alongside others of the same design, distinguished by different-coloured front doors. But the front door of Dean Broad's house was not visible; neither were any of the windows. Not so much as a single brick was exposed to the night air. The house was a heaving mass, covered by so many shifting Severals that it appeared almost alive.

FIFTEEN

Labyrinth

O n Monday morning, Jeb and Cal picked Janey up and made their way to school. Janey met the news of the ginger cat's death with silence, so they walked without talking. Cal was relieved there were no Severals visible in the morning light.

'That doesn't mean they're not close,' said Jeb.

Dean Broad didn't show up for school and Jason Pike sat glumly on his own. Cal made an attempt to ask him how his friend was, but Pike looked startled as he approached and didn't lift his eyes from the desk.

'I dunno. He won't answer the door,' he mumbled. He refused to speak after that.

Lessons passed slowly and when lunchtime finally arrived, Cal peered out from the safety of the school doors. Satisfied the coast was clear, he and Janey moved outside. They stood in a sheltered corner.

'Did the Chattan arrive?' asked Cal.

'I think so. I woke up in the middle of the night and something made me look out of the window, I'm not sure what. I could see a big white cat sitting on one of the cars directly outside the house. It didn't move, just sat there watching the street, like a soldier outside Buckingham Palace. When I looked again this morning, it'd gone.'

'It'll keep out of sight in the day, the Chattan seem very secret.'

'What do you think about Dean not turning up?'

'Not sure,' said Cal. 'We'll tell Dad, but I don't think there's much he can do. Besides, if the ginger Chattan was right, then the Baudouin should be arriving tonight, so maybe he knows more about what's happening.'

A bunch of year sevens wandered over then and they stopped talking. They didn't get another chance to continue their conversation and spent the rest of the day in frustrated silence.

*

During the walk home, Jeb wore the Pod outside his jacket. As daylight turned to dusk, Cal began feeling anxious. But he saw nothing sinister.

Only when Janey had stepped back inside her front gate did Jeb let go of her hand. She ran indoors without looking back. Sitting on a car opposite the house, a large white cat watched them silently.

'His name's Frost,' said Jeb. 'He's a Chattan elder, and

head of his clan. He'll keep a close eye on Janey, don't you worry.'

*

Back on the boat, Cal raised the subject of Dean Broad's absence.

'The Chattan have spotted larger numbers of Severals at the Broad house,' said Jeb. 'Dean's not the only family member affected. His parents haven't been seen since Friday. They're not answering their phone, and anyone ringing the doorbell has been met with silence.'

'How do you know?' asked Cal.

'The Chattan have been watching the house for the last couple of days. They've reported that the Severals' presence is sending visitors away confused and indifferent, most of them not remembering why they'd gone there in the first place.'

'Shouldn't we go and help them?'

'We can't go anywhere near that house,' replied Jeb. 'It's infected.'

'Can't the Pod do anything?'

'No, they're beyond its help. Such is the power of the Mist that once people are turned, it's almost impossible to save them.'

'It's frustrating, Dad. We know things are happening, but we don't know what to do about it.'

'Our priority is to stay safe until Legard arrives. It's not long now, just a few more hours. We *must* be patient. Whatever news he brings will be important.'

'What time will he be at Parliament Hill?'

'I don't know. We'll head there for midnight and wait. I'm sorry to keep you up, but I can't leave you here alone. Not anymore. At least tomorrow's the last day before the Christmas holidays, eh?'

Cal smiled but didn't feel in the least bit festive.

'There's something else I've wanted to ask you about, Dad,' he said eventually.

'What's that?'

'I was wondering about the Labyrinth. Mr Dickens mentioned it and then you talked about it last night. What is it?'

'The Labyrinth is both a blessing and a curse. To be used only in times of dire emergency.'

'Why?' asked Cal.

'Because to enter it is to subject yourself to things more dangerous than those you may be trying to evade,' Jeb replied. 'On one hand, it provides the means for escape, but in the blink of an eye, it can become a trap. It is never, ever to be used lightly. Do you understand?'

'Yes.'

Jeb stood.

'Okay, help me clear some space,' he said.

They moved the furniture to one end of the cabin, leaving the floor clear except for the rug. Jeb crouched down low, allowing Twilight to leap up onto his shoulders.

'I know it makes you nervous, Twilight,' said Jeb, 'but Cal needs to know everything now.'

The Chattan was still but her fur bristled.

'This rug guards the way to the Labyrinth,' said Jeb,

taking a corner of it in his hand. 'And there's a good reason you have never thought to lift it, nor even think about it in all your years on *Podwitch*. That's because a Podhex guards it, ensuring you didn't. It was placed there many years ago.'

With that, he pulled out the Pod and muttered something under his breath. 'Ready?'

Cal nodded and Jeb whipped the rug away.

In the middle of the floor was a trapdoor, perfectly square. Gold hinges ran along one edge, and at the opposite end a gold handle, smooth and shiny, lay against the wood. There were no locks or bolts of any kind.

'This is a Labyrinth gateway.'

'Where does it go?'

'Anywhere and everywhere.'

Jeb stepped forward, motioning Cal to one side. He gripped the handle, heaving the trapdoor upward. Cal winced, half expecting something to come swooping up from beneath it. But nothing did. The door opened without a sound and Jeb stood over it, looking down. Cal waited before inching forward to join him.

A shaft dropped away from the opening, just big enough for an adult to squeeze through. Its stone walls were damp and crumbling in places. A ladder made of dull grey metal descended on one side. The light from the cabin penetrated no more than ten rungs down and beyond that the shaft was plunged into darkness. A strange smell, musty and stale, reached up, borne on an icy breeze that chilled Cal to the bone.

Twilight mewed quietly from Jeb's shoulder.

'Down there is a network of passageways that lead anywhere in the world, no matter how near or far,' said Jeb. 'It can take you the fifteen-minute walk to school or all the way to Africa if you choose. There are endless miles of tunnels criss-crossing without logic or reason, and no way of knowing which to follow. The only safe way to navigate it is by carrying the Pod, which will become bright, lighting your way as soon as you enter. It will remain so, as long as you take the right path to your desired destination. Take a wrong turn and the Pod will dim in warning, lighting up again only when you select the right path once more.'

'How did it come to be there?'

'It's said to have existed since the beginning of the world. No one knows who built it or why. It has become a place used by both good and evil, walked by those desperate enough for whom the dangers above ground are too great. It is not a refuge but a place of travel, and many that wander its depths have been known never to re-emerge. There are bad things down there, Cal. The stuff of nightmares. For a long time, it was a prison to the Severals. Your grandmother, one of the most powerful Aldhelm to have lived, trapped them there. Now they have escaped for the first time in decades, and it's happened on my watch.'

Jeb paused for a moment and swallowed before speaking.

'Some say it was once the lair of the Nephilim, a refuge created by them. What I *do* know is that to travel the Labyrinth without a Pod at your side would be madness.

I have only used it once. I swore then that I would not pass through it again unless in an absolute emergency.'

A noise, ever so slight, followed by a faint echo, sounded somewhere deep below.

'Stand back!' Jeb hissed, lifting the door with his foot and slamming it shut.

He slid the rug back in place and took a corner of it in his hand, the other grasping the Pod as his mouth moved silently. After a moment, he turned to Cal, breathing heavily.

'It's safe now. Let's put the furniture back.'

*

Later, Cal found himself unable to focus on the rug at all. No matter how hard he tried, his eyes just sort of slipped over it. He knew the gateway was there but to think of it was difficult, almost impossible.

'How long has it been there, Dad?'

'It's always been part of *Podwitch*, long before we arrived in London. You see, she was built at a time when people lived and worked on narrowboats all over the world.

'The Aldhelm who built *Podwitch* was the last of his bloodline, and he built her to allow him to continue his work on the canals while undertaking his role as Pod Guardian. He used Podmagic to create the gateway, building it as part of the boat so that no matter where *Podwitch* is moored, if it is opened, the shaft will take you down to the Labyrinth, allowing you to go wherever you need. It was a masterstroke, meaning that even if the boat's protection fails, allowing her to be boarded, there is always an escape route.'

Jeb moved his hands in wide gestures as he spoke.

'Ever since, *Podwitch* has passed from each Aldhelm to the next, some choosing to live on her, others simply mooring her up and using her when needed.' Jeb paused before continuing. 'But there is one last thing you should know, Cal. You'll have noted that there are no locks on the gateway.'

Cal nodded.

'If the Podhex should ever be broken, the protection preventing access to the outside of the boat does not cover us inside. We'd be susceptible to anything in the Labyrinth that wanted to find us.'

Cal pictured something clambering out of the darkness, one rung at a time, until it arrived just beneath the trapdoor, separated from them only by a few centimetres of wood. He shivered at the thought.

SIXTEEN

Salutations And Pursuit

———————

Hours later, Cal stared at the vista of London as stars sparkled in the sky above, appearing to reflect the sea of electric lights that stretched as far as the eye could see. Glass buildings shaped like giant vegetables nestled alongside tired concrete tower blocks. There was a chill in the air, hinting at more frost-tinged mornings to come, and with dawn close by, a full moon still glowed in the cloudless sky.

Jeb's breath billowed in clouds as he gripped his old pocket watch in rigid fingers. Its ornate face was clearly visible in the moonlight, a magnet for his eyes, that seemed to draw them with increasing rapidity as each second passed. He raised a hand to where Twilight balanced on his shoulder, nestling against his cheek. Flicking the watch shut, he slid it into the pocket of his waistcoat and blew on his hands.

'Have you met the Baudouin before?' Cal asked him.

'No, it's unusual for Guardians to meet each other.'

'So how will we know it's him?'

'Don't worry, Cal. We'll know. Now go and wait a little further back. I want to make absolutely sure of things before he knows you're here.'

CRACK!

Somewhere close by, a twig snapped. A figure was making its way up the hill towards them.

'Hurry, Cal. Move!'

Cal retreated several paces and watched through the leaves of the bush he'd hidden behind.

The approaching figure was an elderly man with a walking stick. He stopped when just ten feet of grass separated him from Jeb. Without speaking, he withdrew a metal chain from around his neck. He lifted it over his head and let the small orb that hung there dangle from his fingers. Jeb eyed it cautiously before reaching inside his jumper to withdraw his own.

Lights began to glow at the centres of the two orbs, one a deep warm red, the second a rich, familiar blue. Each Guardian studied the other's Pod intently, the colours reflecting brightly in their eyes.

'Cool,' murmured Cal. 'Janey would love this.'

Slowly the lights began to fade. Placing the chains back over their heads, the men stepped forward and shook each other warmly by the hand.

'My name is Jeb, Jeb Wainwright. Welcome to London.'

Cal knew then that all was well. The Baudouin had arrived. Jeb turned to him, beckoning him forward.

'And this is my son, Cal.'

'*Enchanté*,' replied the Baudouin, regarding him carefully. '*Je m'appelle Jean Legard.*' He reached a hand to Twilight and she nuzzled against his fingers. '*Ça va, ma belle?*' he said, smiling as she purred loudly.

Turning to the view, he continued, speaking in a thick French accent.

'So it begins, Aldhelm. I had a feeling it would be here in London, but did not think I would live to see it.'

'I only wish it'd been in someone else's time,' said Jeb.

'Oh, but, Monsieur Wainwright, if only,' replied the Baudouin.

'We should get out of the open,' said Jeb.

Cal saw a flicker of concern cross the Frenchman's face.

'My home is less than an hour on foot if that's okay?' continued Jeb. 'Only Cal and I live there. The protection is strong, and we have a stove.'

Jean Legard listened, considering the offer before nodding, grateful at the thought of warmth and shelter. Jeb lifted Twilight from his shoulder and placed her gently on the ground.

'Now, old girl, we must get a message to Monsieur Legard's Chattan in Paris.'

Twilight swung her golden eyes towards the Frenchman.

'Her name is Hibou,' said Monsieur Legard. 'She will be waiting at the base of the Tour Eiffel between midnight and one o'clock each night until she receives news. She must know that I have met with the Aldhelm and will return soon. I will send word to her when I leave London.'

Twilight waited, ensuring that he had finished, then jumped up and twined herself through Jeb's legs before skipping lightly into the undergrowth.

'Be careful,' Jeb called, watching her disappear. He turned back to Monsieur Legard. 'We should be going. There is much to discuss and time is short.'

Setting off towards the bright lights and grubby Camden streets, Jeb walked briskly, hands in his pockets and head down, with Cal at his side. Legard kept up, surprisingly agile for an older man. His walking stick tapped on the path, setting a rhythm to their pace. When they were clear of the heath, they moved through smaller side streets whenever possible. Descending through Chalk Farm towards Camden, they passed under the railway bridge that spanned the main road before turning into a cobbled street that was home to the market, normally packed in the daytime but now deserted.

'Not far now,' said Jeb.

Cal glanced over his shoulder as an ambulance raced along the high street behind them, lights flashing and siren screeching. He was about to turn back when a fleeting movement caught his eye, a brief shimmer that passed the end of the cobbled street where it fronted the main road. There it was again! This time, it was unmistakable, a shapeless shadow, moving quickly.

'Dad!' he whispered as loudly as he dared.

But Jeb had already stopped and swung around, his hand reaching for the Pod, eyes blazing.

The click of Monsieur Legard's cane receded behind them then stopped as the old man realised they were no longer moving. An unnatural silence had descended, replacing the distant rumble of traffic. Silence smothered the area like a blanket of snow.

It was then that the Severals came, flooding around the corners of the buildings. They writhed and twisted together as they moved.

'*Mon Dieu!*' cried Monsieur Legard, his cane crashing to the floor.

Jeb yanked the Pod from his overcoat, its blue light blazing powerfully. As the light spread, those Severals nearest to it disintegrated with a sharp hiss. The others, surging behind, stopped and hung silently, avoiding its touch. A huge pressure forced him backwards, but Jeb never let his eyes leave the wall of shadows in front of him. Shapeless and faceless, they continued pouring into the street, some clinging to the walls of buildings, while others skulked close to the cobbles, seeking a way around the Podlight.

Just as Cal thought Jeb would collapse under the strain, the blue light was joined by a radiant red as Jean Legard appeared next to him, his own Pod adding reinforcement.

'I have never seen so many,' muttered the Frenchman.

'We can't stay here,' said Jeb. 'Home is close by. Are you able to run?'

'*Oui.*'

The two men lifted the chains over their heads and held the Pods up high, ensuring that they left no gaps in the light for the Severals to attack.

'Stay in single file. Cal, you're in the middle.'

Cal and Monsieur Legard nodded.

'Go!' cried Jeb.

They were off and running. The Severals moved quickly after them, toying with the blue and red light, leaping forward and then back as the Pods thrashed about in the darkness. Jeb led them behind the deserted market space, descending the stone steps to the canal as Severals swarmed around them.

Cal heard a sudden cry behind him and turned to see Monsieur Legard sprawled on the ground. His Pod lay dark on the concrete next to him.

'Dad!' cried Cal.

But Jeb was hemmed in, his blue light pulsing amidst the twisted shapes. Cal moved without thinking and ran back to where the old man lay, scrabbling for his Pod. He could feel the Severals surround him and his thoughts began to cloud. From somewhere in the distance, he could hear Jeb calling his name. Cal shook himself and reached down to pull the Baudouin up.

Just as the Frenchman's fingers connected with his Pod, Jeb leapt into their midst, his Podlight spreading the Severals around them like flies. Legard lifted his own, a surge of red light returning to it at his touch.

'Are you all right?' cried Jeb.

'Yes!' shouted Cal.

Then they were away again, running once more.

Severals thronged the canal, pouring down from the overhead streets. Ahead, by the base of the steep concrete walls, the collection of narrowboats nestled at the edge of the towpath.

'Just a little further,' Jeb panted.

And then they were at *Podwitch* and crossing the gangplank. Moments later, the Severals were all around the boat. Its protective layer, like a giant bubble, was being battered on all sides. They scratched at it and beat at it with their fists, but it held firm.

Inside the barrier, the deafening silence had lifted, and the normal rumble of the city returned. The Podlights grew dull, their protection no longer needed.

Monsieur Legard could not speak, instead simply lowering himself to the wooden deck. Cal's chest burned as though it was on fire, and he took great gulps of air as he stared at the Severals surrounding them.

Jeb moved to the wooden doors and swung them open.

'Welcome aboard our humble home,' he said, gesturing towards the warm light within.

Monsieur Legard took a last look at the throng of shadows pushing angrily at the protective barrier before stepping down into the boat. Cal followed, and then Jeb, closing the wooden doors behind him.

SEVENTEEN

Yesterday's Betrayal, Today's Undertaking

Jeb lifted a curtain and glanced out. Early morning light had just begun to crown the sky in gold. The area immediately surrounding *Podwitch* and its narrowboat neighbours was clear, without a Several to be seen. Jeb let the curtain drop and turned back to the Baudouin, nodding and shooting him a tight smile.

'How about some proper introductions? Cal, meet the Baudouin, Monsieur Legard. Monsieur Legard, this is my son and the future Aldhelm, Cal.'

The Baudouin had removed his hat and stood facing Cal. He was of medium build, well dressed in smart blue trousers and shiny brown leather shoes. Under his overcoat he wore a blue blazer and white shirt with a yellow necktie. His white hair was swept back neatly, almost reaching his shoulders. His face was lined with age, coloured by ruddy cheeks. His eyes were bright and full of kindness.

'*Bonjour, Cal,*' he said.

'*Bonjour, Monsieur Legard,*' Cal replied.

They shook hands and the Baudouin looked at him solemnly.

'Now listen,' said Monsieur Legard. 'We need to put an important rule in place, which is to call each other only by our first names. After all, I know we will become good friends, *non*? So please, call me Jean.'

A smile broke across the Frenchman's face and, despite his age, he was neither arrogant nor teacherly, and spoke to Cal as an equal. Cal warmed to him immediately.

'*Bonjour, Jean,*' he said, smiling.

'Sorry it's a little cramped,' said Jeb. 'We don't have many guests on *Podwitch*.'

'*Mais non,*' Jean Legard replied. 'Your home is perfect, very cosy. Besides, the reputation of *Podwitch* is well known amongst Pod Guardians. There is more to this *petit bateau* than meets the eye, *n'est ce pas*?'

'Absolutely,' said Jeb. 'She's our home and our refuge.'

'*Parfait!* Now how about some *chocolat chaud*?'

Soon the three of them were drinking hot chocolate and eating toasted muffins smothered in melted butter.

'So, Jean, I need to know what's happening,' said Jeb.

'You've kept a low profile for days. I assume you know that the Labyrinth has been breached.'

Legard nodded but said nothing.

'Things in London are going badly. The ravens at the Tower were killed, the Severals have become bold, and my own Nephilim has appeared, once directly, to threaten Cal.'

Legard's eyes darted to Cal at the mention of his name.

'The focus appears to be London itself,' continued Jeb, 'although I have yet to find where the Labyrinth has been breached. As you've witnessed tonight, the Severals are confident, and the Chattan messenger that delivered news of your coming was attacked and killed.'

Legard's eyes widened at this and he shook his head slightly before speaking.

'Things have become so bad I feared even to contact you,' he said. 'There is a chance even the Chattan have been infiltrated. The news of my coming to London was too important to fall into the wrong hands, but it seems as if the Nephilim already knew. We are lucky the messenger made it here at all, *non*?'

'Things must be bad if we suspect the Chattan cannot be trusted,' said Jeb.

'Oh, things are bad, Jeb,' said Legard. 'Have you communicated with the Blue Plaque Network?'

'Yes, with Dickens.'

'Ah, *bon*, a good man.'

'He told us a little of the chaos that he suspects is coming.'

'*C'est vrai*,' replied Legard. He looked at Cal. 'It's true,' he added with a brief smile. 'My Nephilim, his name is Cain, visited me eight days ago. It had been more than thirty years since I saw him. The last time our paths crossed we fought, and I left him for dead. It took every ounce of willpower for me to refrain from taking his life back then. I pray to this day that it will not turn out to be my greatest mistake.'

Jeb looked puzzled. 'But if he was killed, you'd die too. A Pod Guardian cannot exist without their Nephilim, you know that,' he said.

'*Bien sûr, mon ami*,' replied the Frenchman, his eyes heavy. 'But there have been times, in my darker moments, when I have considered that perhaps it would be worth my life to rid the world of him. Even for a Nephilim, Cain reaches depths others cannot imagine.'

'No!' said Jeb sharply. 'That goes against everything the Guardians stand for.'

His eyes locked with those of the older man. Legard's face was calm.

'Nevertheless, it is one of the great burdens we must carry, *non*? To be, in some way, responsible for their existence.'

Jeb looked away.

'What did he say?' Cal interrupted.

'He spent some time recounting the tale of our first encounter many years ago,' replied Legard. 'My family were killed when France was invaded by Germany in 1940. When the Germans arrived at our farmhouse, my father, the Baudouin before me, put the Pod in my hands.

He told me to run and keep it safe. I did so and I left them, all of them, with the sound of gunfire rattling in my ears. But there was one who pursued me, just one.'

Legard hesitated, caught up in the memory for a moment.

'I knew he was chasing me, and I ran until I felt my lungs would explode, holding the Pod so tightly that the metal chain bit into my flesh. I was convinced that I had lost him. At last, in the dead of night, I crawled into a deserted barn and collapsed in the hay. I was exhausted and had wept so many tears that my eyes were now dry. My only thoughts were with those I had left behind.'

'What happened next?' asked Cal.

'I suppose I would have fallen asleep, had I not felt the cold kiss of a gun barrel against my head. There he was, as bright and fresh as when I had glimpsed him at the farm. There was no way he could have reached that barn before me. I was covered in mud and soaked to the skin. But upon his uniform there was not the slightest mark, and not one bead of sweat was there upon his skin. I knew then he was not German, that it was just a disguise. He was not even human.'

Jeb leaned against the kitchen worktop, his face grave. Legard continued.

'Cain introduced himself to me as the one who was to wander the earth as my shadow. He told me of the power of the Mist and how, within months, the world would succumb to its greatness. He knew my inner secrets and fears, and laughed at my apprehension. He mocked the death of my father, telling me that it was nothing compared to the true sorrow that was to come. I was helpless in front of him, and greatly ashamed.'

Legard paused and took the Pod between his fingers.

'Then I remembered this little orb that my father had passed to me. I could feel it beginning to throb with life under my palm. Its warmth was a comfort to me. When I opened my fingers, its bright red light was shining fiercely. I glanced at Cain and saw fear in his eyes, and then he was gone. He disappeared, like a wolf abandoning a newborn lamb, scared off after wasting time playing and not completing the kill. I lay in the hay feeling safe for the first time that day. Eventually, the light faded, but not before exhaustion consumed me and I slept.' Legard sighed and shook his head. 'It is all history, and much has happened since then.'

'What made him approach you now?' asked Jeb.

'He has changed since I last saw him. While I have grown old, it seems he has become younger, stronger. I fear, should it come to it, that I would have no chance in direct combat with him now. My strength is not what it used to be. After he was done with mocking my grey hairs and wrinkled skin, he warned me of a new coming of the Mist. Fire danced in his eyes and he laughed as he showed me visions of Hitler's war, revelling in the devastation they had wrought, of how close they had come to succeeding. He said that things had gone badly for them back then, but their time is coming again. They have grown strong.'

Legard paused for a moment and took a mouthful of hot chocolate before continuing.

'Your mother was a legend amongst Pod Guardians, Jeb. Despite her youth, her work in holding back the tide that flooded through Europe at that time is famous. To those in the so-called real world, the Battle of Britain is how things are remembered, and it is true that men and women fought and died more bravely than most of us could possibly imagine. But, for those in the world of Pods, another battle was being fought unseen. It was your mother who did much to save England, and possibly the rest of Europe when all was against her. It was she who masterminded the trapping of the Severals in the Labyrinth. What good was I, one of her closest allies, to her? I was new to my responsibilities, afraid and helpless.'

Jeb frowned. 'I know all this, Jean. Mother's work speaks for itself. But what has it got to do with what's happening now?'

Jean Legard sighed. His eyes were watery.

'There was a man, a human, who betrayed Churchill, when he had become prime minister. This man sold his secrets to the Nephilim, almost allowing them to gain victory. His name was Gretchley, Edmund Gretchley. The Nephilim used the Severals to poison this man's mind, and due to his position in government, he was able to pass on secrets and information that they would not have otherwise known.'

Jeb was leaning forward now, suddenly interested.

'One night, when the Germans were closer than ever to crushing Britain, your mother discovered the traitor's identity. She was only just in time to save the prime minister and get him to safety, averting an unthinkable catastrophe.'

Jean Legard smiled sadly and paused.

'We Guardians are not afforded great margins between success and failure. It is true she masterminded the capture of the Severals and the submission of the Nephilim, but at the last moment, Gretchley slipped through her fingers. Allowing him to escape was her biggest failure.'

'Why?' asked Jeb quietly.

'This man, who has been in hiding for all these years, has returned. It is he who has used his knowledge to open the Labyrinth and free the Severals. It is he who has made contact with the Nephilim, he who is hungry for power once more.'

'Could one man do all that?' asked Cal.

'*Mais oui*, Cal. And more importantly, it seems he has come home. Cain confirmed that the centre for this new storm was to be here, in London. Gretchley has awoken the Nephilim and made them hungry once more. Made them believe. Now you understand why I had to come.'

Jeb was silent.

'But surely we can find him and stop him?' said Cal. 'He's only a man, isn't he? He must be really old too.'

'If only that were true,' sighed Legard, 'but we have no idea who he is. His identity is changed, and the Pods can only warn us when agents of the Mist are close, such as the Nephilim or the Severals. This man is free to act as he likes, and yet he is the one who is the true danger.'

'But how did he work out how to open the Labyrinth?'

Legard shrugged and sat back.

'*Je ne sais pas, mes amis.* On that I have no answer. I have shared all I know.'

Jeb shook his head, frowning.

'Why would Cain warn you? Why tell you of the Mist, of Gretchley, let alone give away the focus on London? It doesn't make sense.'

'*Bof!*' exclaimed the Frenchman. 'Cain has always been something of a... how do you say... a bragger? He is arrogant and believes telling me will make little difference. Who knows, perhaps he is right. After all, we have little time to prepare. I am surprised you got my message at all. Even the cat paid with his life, *non*? And what advantage has it given us? *Rien.* None.'

It was true, Cal thought. Even Mr Dickens had not been able to offer much, needing to seek more advice before knowing what to do.

'But why are you here, Jean? If London is the true focus, then this is my fight, until it spreads beyond England's borders,' said Jeb.

'Because, my friend, I recall how helpless I was in the years when your mother stood alone. I could do nothing back then. Perhaps if I had been stronger, I might have been able to help her, and Gretchley would not have escaped. I have never forgiven myself for failing her. Now I will make amends. And two is better than one, *non*?'

'And three's better than two,' said Cal quietly.

'*C'est vrai*,' repeated Legard, giving him a warm smile. 'It's true. I cannot leave Paris unprotected for too long, but will do all I can.'

'Given what you've said, our first concern should be

for Dickens,' said the Aldhelm. 'I've heard nothing from him for several days. He was supposed to contact me. The Severals have managed to cross to the place outside time. They found us, even there.'

'What?' said Legard, leaning forward in his chair. '*C'est pas possible.*'

'Until now, it seems,' said Jeb.

The old man sat back. 'We must find a way to recontact the Plaque Network, no question,' he said.

'I've been trying but the Podmap won't react. Either they can't be ready to talk yet, or…'

'Or?'

'Perhaps the Nephilim have found a way to block their attempts to contact us,' said Jeb.

'True enough, but do not forget we now have the strength of two Pods, which should be more than enough to break through whatever may be preventing them.'

Legard swung his Pod from side to side, a mischievous glint in his eye, and Jeb smiled.

'It's worth a go, I guess, but it's going to have to wait for now.'

'Come on, Dad, why?' said Cal.

'Because we have to get you and Janey to school. It's the last day before the Christmas holidays and almost eight o'clock in the morning.'

EIGHTEEN

On The Run

Monsieur Legard accompanied Cal and Jeb to Janey's house.

'Are you sure you don't want to rest?' asked Jeb.

'*Mais non*, I feel fine, younger than I look!' he winked.

The three of them stepped out from *Podwitch* into a bright morning. Cal's eyes roamed the towpath for any sign of movement.

'Dusk and darkness is the Severals' time,' said Legard, laying a comforting hand on his shoulder.

Old Mr Bentley was in his deckchair, wrapped in a large fleece jacket, soaking up the winter sun. He nodded at them, eyeing Legard with suspicion typical of an elderly neighbour.

'Morning, Mr Bentley,' called Jeb, raising a hand in greeting.

'Jeb, Cal,' the old man replied, nodding. 'Lovely day,' he added.

Cal was just happy to be in sunshine once more, free of the menace that had been building over the last week.

Janey ran down her front steps to meet them, introducing herself to Monsieur Legard with a beaming smile.

'We've been waiting ages for you to arrive!' she said brightly.

Legard lifted his hat in greeting before shaking her firmly by the hand.

'*Enchanté*,' he said.

The Pod Guardians left the children at the school gates, watching until they had entered the building safely.

Lessons were more relaxed with the onset of the festive season, but dragged on as usual. When the morning break finally arrived, Cal led Janey to a corner of the playground and filled her in on the night's events. Her eyes shone as she listened.

'That Mr Legard is well cool!' she said.

'Yeah, he seems nice too,' said Cal. 'Kind of wise. I mean, I think Dad's clever but because Monsieur Legard has been around for longer, he seems more sure of himself. Dad needs his help.'

'Yeah, well, those Nephi-thingies don't scare me one bit. The scariest thing about Thorne was the state of his nails. He could use a good bath. We should dunk him in the canal, that'd do the trick!'

Cal smiled, remembering how petrified the two of them had really been, but he was glad for Janey's bravado.

At that moment, he realised how lonely life would be if she wasn't around.

*

When the school bell rang at the end of the afternoon, corridors reverberated with the sound of running feet and slamming doors. The last stream of kids ran across the playground in the brackish gloom. Free for Christmas and two weeks off school, Cal and Janey made their way to the front gates.

The Severals were conspicuous in their absence.

Jeb and Monsieur Legard were approaching up the slight incline of the street towards them. Jeb raised a hand in greeting. Cal waved back, noticing that the Baudouin had a new walking stick. He could hear it clicking against the pavement as they approached.

'*Bonsoir, mes enfants!*' the Frenchman called out.

'Hi!' replied Janey.

'Good day?' asked Jeb.

Cal noticed how tired he looked. His eyes were circled in darkness, and his skin was pale.

'The usual,' muttered Janey. 'I'm just happy it's over and now it's time for the holidays!'

A lone car growled out of the school gates, behind them.

'Come on then, let's not stand about.'

They walked side by side, the children flanked by the Guardians. Christmas lights flashed in windows, splashing happy thoughts onto the murky street.

Cal wasn't sure whether it was the sound of the walking stick or their shoes against the pavement that disappeared first, but instantly the distant drone of the city became silent. The Pod Guardians exchanged glances and then scoured the street, their bodies tense.

'Dad, what is it?' whispered Cal.

'Shhh!' replied Jean Legard, listening intently. 'Jeb, stay with the children.'

The Baudouin stepped into the road and turned slowly, letting his eyes explore the street. Cal felt the comfort of Jeb's hand on his shoulder. Jean Legard reached into his jacket and pulled out the Pod. He held it briefly before letting it dangle lifelessly from his fingers. He stared at it before striding back towards them.

'Give Cal your Pod, Jeb,' he said quietly.

'What?' said the Aldhelm.

Legard held up his Pod. There was no light; the little orb was grey and dull.

'The Podmagic has been blocked. They cannot protect us here. We have no choice. We must give them to the children.'

Jeb's eyes widened and he knelt in front of Cal.

'Take it,' he said urgently. 'Take it and put it on. Quickly!'

Jeb grabbed Cal's hand, pressing the Pod into it. A muted blue flash sparked briefly in recognition before it gave up and faded to nothing. Cal hesitated, clenching his hand tightly around it.

'Hurry!' Jean pleaded. 'You have to trust me.' He stared at Cal before lifting his own chain over his head.

He held the Pod out to Janey, and she took it gently and placed it around her neck, tucking it inside her coat.

Legard took the children by their shoulders and crouched down in front of them.

'We'll do what we can to slow them down,' he said. 'Hopefully, you'll have time to make it to *Podwitch*.'

Jeb stood close by. His face was lined with worry.

'Cal, the Pod *will* respond to you when you get it away from here,' he said. 'Remember, it reacts to your touch and you *must* use it to access the Podmap. We made a breakthrough today. Dickens is ready to speak. He'll be able to help you.'

'But, Dad... I...' Cal stammered.

'There's no time for talking,' said Jeb firmly. 'Use the book. It will tell you what you need to know. Now go.'

A sound, like gas escaping from a ruptured pipe, came from somewhere along the pavement. Cal recognised Thorne's laughter immediately. Janey gasped and grabbed his hand, squeezing his fingers tightly. A look of apprehension crossed Jeb's face, but he winked at them.

'Go,' he mouthed.

Cal pulled Janey by the hand and ran.

*

'Let the children go!' Thorne's voice sliced through the air behind them. 'We have the two we need.'

Around him, Severals were emerging from their camouflage as paving slabs or car hub caps, while others materialised out of the darkening sky to hang from streetlamps and squat on car roofs, noiseless and menacing.

Revulsion flooded through Cal as another hiss of laughter chased them along the pavement, mocking their every step. He looked straight ahead, thinking only of his dad and Jean Legard.

He ducked into an alleyway, pulling Janey with him, then stopped to peer back at where the Pod Guardians stood before Thorne. The Nephilim was smiling at them. It was a smile that promised pain.

'Can you see anything?' asked Janey, breathing hard behind him.

The Nephilim stepped forward, licking his lips. He raised a hand and a group of Severals grabbed the Guardians, forcing them to their knees. A smile played on Thorne's face as he tore open Jeb's coat. His talons raked across the Aldhelm's chest, causing him to cry out in pain. On seeing the empty space at Jeb's neck where the Pod should have been, the Nephilim hissed angrily.

'What's going on, Cal?' Janey asked, hopping from one foot to the other. 'What was that noise?'

Thorne moved across to Legard and flung open his overcoat. Seeing no Pod at the Baudouin's neck, he struck him across the face, sending the old man crashing to the ground. The Nephilim howled, a deafening wail that cut through Cal's skin, tearing at the bones beneath. He then turned to the sea of throbbing shadows and spread his arms wide, drawing his hands from the pockets of his coat.

'Severals of Carden!' he cried out. 'Soon it will be

time to gorge yourselves on the human world once more. Your patience over these past decades will be rewarded. I promise you feasting until there are none left upon which to feed.'

The assembled mass grew frenzied and sniffed the air excitedly.

'But first, I command you to seek out the Aldhelm's child, and his little friend. Hunt them down and stop at nothing to trace them. They cannot be far.'

The Severals swarmed, vaulting over garden walls and squeezing under gates, slithering up steps to doors and windows. They crawled over one another, pushing themselves through letterboxes and under loose roof tiles.

Cal and Janey set off again, quickly coming to the opposite end of the alleyway.

'This street's empty,' said Cal, looking out. They moved into it, heading towards the junction at one end and the street on which Janey lived. 'I'm gonna drop you off at your place, where you should be safe. Then I'll go to *Podwitch*,' he added, trying to inject calm into his voice.

'No way, Cal. I'm coming with you.' Janey stopped and stared at him fiercely. 'You're not going anywhere without me.'

'Janey,' Cal said in a warning tone.

'What?'

'Remember what Dad said? You had to do whatever he or I said at all times. Come on, we're wasting time. The Severals will be here any minute.'

'I don't care what he said, Cal. You can't deal with this on your own. Until we find out what they've done with your dad and Jean, you're going to need help, right?'

Cal was thrown by her logic. His mind kept returning to the image of his dad kneeling in front of Thorne, the claw marks carved into his chest. As he hovered, countless numbers of Severals were attacking people's homes, doing God knows what to those who lived there as they searched for him and Janey. He tried to think but his head spun maniacally, forcing him towards despair.

'Cal!' Janey's voice shocked him.

He looked at her, thinking fast.

'Okay,' he said. 'We'll stick together, but from now on we go with my decisions. Got it?'

'Done,' she said.

For a brief moment, Cal was close to throwing his arms around her, relieved that she wasn't going to abandon him. But movement at the top of the street caught his eye as hundreds of shapes swarmed into it, covering buildings and cars. He grabbed Janey's hand and began running again as the agitated sniffing of the Severals grew louder behind them.

'Where are we going?' cried Janey.

'Your place, we don't have a choice. At least it's protected. We can think properly there,' Cal panted, instinct taking over.

A groan came from behind them; the Severals had caught their scent. Whipping his head round, Cal saw they were moving quickly, closing the gap. He ran even faster, tightening his grip on Janey's hand.

As they entered the street, the insistent snorting had neared to within a few paces of them.

'Come on!' Cal shouted. 'Nearly there!'

Nails scrabbled at his shirt, causing him to lunge forward. As they neared Janey's house, he pulled her in front of him, flinging her towards the gate. She fumbled at the latch as Cal felt arctic fingers grab his collar, yanking him backwards off his feet.

'Cal!' Janey screamed.

His fall was broken by his school bag.

'Stay where you are, Janey!' he called out.

Throbbing shapes tightened around him. But before they could close in, a blood-curdling screech pierced the darkness.

Cal looked up. As he did so, a gap opened in the shadowy throng and he saw, to his amazement, the frenzied movement of a large white house cat. It slashed this way and that at the shadows, spitting fiercely. The Severals pulled away from it but it leapt at them, tearing the darkness from those it could reach.

In a split second, Cal was up and running through the Severals, jumping and clearing Janey's garden wall in a single leap. Turning, he watched the dark shapes heaving angrily, turning their heads for a scent of him.

'Cal, thank God!' Janey cried.

'It's okay, I'm fine.'

His eyes sought out the Chattan that had come to their aid. As they watched, one of the Severals slid forward, wrenching the cat to the ground. Together, they slashed and bit at one another in a ferocious struggle.

'Inside,' Cal said, turning to Janey.

'But what about Frost?'

'There's nothing we can do. Come on!'

Janey had the keys in her hand before they reached the top of the steps and they moved quickly through the front door, slamming it shut behind them. Janey's fingers shook as she worked the key and bolts. When she had drawn them across, the children sank to the floor, their backs against the door and the nightmare hordes outside.

NINETEEN

Comes The Gloaming

'Poor Frost, I don't think he stood a chance out there,' said Janey. Her voice was shaking. 'What are we gonna do?'

Cal closed his eyes, fighting an overwhelming urge to burst into tears. His chest heaved as he waited, letting the emotion retreat, then he turned to look Janey in the eye.

'If I can get Dad's Pod to work, we may be able to get help through the map.'

He stood and peered through the letterbox.

'What can you see?' Janey asked.

The usual early evening activity of cars and people was absent. No lights shone from the houses. The whole street pulsed beneath countless shadows.

'This is the only house the Severals haven't touched. The protection must be working. I think we're safe.'

'Thank God,' said Janey.

Cal slammed the letterbox.

'Shhh!' hissed Janey. 'They'll hear you!'

'They're blind and deaf, remember?'

'Oh yeah, I forgot.'

They stood awkwardly. Cal was out of ideas.

'I could use a warm drink while we're thinking,' said Janey. 'You want something?'

'Got any hot chocolate? I can't stop shaking.'

'Yeah, come through to the kitchen.'

She turned on the hall light.

'Leave it off,' said Cal, flinching. 'Just in case Thorne turns up.'

'Sorry.'

Janey flicked the switch, and they crept through to the kitchen. Cal sat at the table as Janey felt her way around in the half-light.

'This is weird,' she said before Cal heard a bang, followed by, 'Ouch! Dammit!'

'You okay?' he asked.

'Yeah, just hit my knee on the table leg.'

He sat back down and put his head in his hands, listening to the sound of spoons clinking against mugs. Part of him wanted to throw the front door open and run to *Podwitch*, but he remembered the night of the car crash and how the Severals had made him feel. There was no choice but to wait and think carefully about what to do next.

He took out the Pod, examining its dull greyness. Why had it stopped working? Had his dad been expecting an ambush? If so, why had he said nothing?

Janey pushed a steaming mug in front of him. He

cupped it in his hands, letting the warmth flow through his arms to the rest of his body.

'It's funny,' he said.

'What is?'

'Just a few days ago, I almost hated Dad for trying to involve me in something I didn't want to believe. Now I don't know what I'd do if I lost him.'

Tears stung his eyes and he fought against them. If Janey noticed, she said nothing. He wiped a hand across his face, trying to clear his head.

'When are your parents due back?' he asked.

'It's Thursday so Mum's working late. She won't be back before eight. Dad's away in Europe with work.'

'Good,' said Cal, looking at the kitchen clock. 'It's five thirty so we've got time, but you're gonna have to leave her a note telling her you're safe with me. Say you're staying on *Podwitch* tonight and that we'll drop you off tomorrow. Will she go for that?'

'She's gonna have to,' said Janey, pulling a pen and pad from a drawer under the table. She hesitated and looked at Cal, concern etched on her face. 'She'll be okay, won't she? Out there, I mean, with all the Severals. There are so many of them.'

Cal shrugged and Janey nodded, her face glum.

'What did you see, Cal? What did they do to your dad and Jean?'

'Nothing,' he replied, a little too quickly. 'I couldn't really see much. They were just talking.'

'I'm sure they're okay,' Janey added, watching him closely.

Cal nodded and took a big gulp of hot chocolate. He was grateful for a distraction.

They sat in silence, each isolated in their own despair, before a distant noise caught their attention. It was the sound of raised voices coming from the street. Cal motioned for Janey to stay where she was and tiptoed into the hallway, trailing a hand along the wall. He pushed open the living room door and stepped inside.

The darkness of the room reminded Cal of a hushed cinema, and the bay window overlooking the front garden resembled a giant screen. He approached it slowly.

On the opposite side of the street stood four people; local residents in the middle of an animated conversation about where one of them had parked their car. None of them had the slightest awareness of the swarm of dark forms surrounding them. As Cal watched, their movements became more agitated. Soon two of the people, both women, were standing nose-to-nose, hurling abuse at one another. Severals all along the street raced towards them, pushing and jostling to get nearer.

Cal's eyes glanced at the small porcelain dog on the windowsill in front of him. He prayed the Podmagic would hold strong until they could form a plan.

A scream caused him to look up and he saw the two women were now involved in a violent struggle. They were pulling hair and scratching at faces, hurling wild insults at each other. Within seconds, the others, two men this time, had started their own battle and fierce punches were flying. Cal noticed that some of the Severals had gripped the people's limbs in their hands, controlling them like puppets. They hurled the humans at one another furiously as their voices cursed and screamed.

Cal heard a sob behind him. He turned to see Janey, her hands covering her mouth in shock as she watched her neighbours punch, kick and bite each other in uncontrolled fury. He pulled her into the hallway, closing the door behind them. The sounds of the struggle grew dim but still remained, relentless and brutal.

'I said stay in the kitchen, didn't I?'

'I know… I'm sorry, Cal. It's just I heard a noise at the back door.'

'What did it sound like?'

'A sort of scrabbling, as though something was trying to get in. It started, then went quiet, then started again.'

Cal swallowed and walked towards the kitchen. He stood in the doorway and listened.

'I can't hear anything now,' he said.

He took Janey's hand, and they moved into the room. Halfway to the back door, Janey stopped.

'Come on,' Cal said. 'We're safe in the house, remember?'

He prayed he was right and inched forward. When they were three feet from the door, a scrabbling sound came from the other side of it. Cal froze.

'That's it!' whispered Janey, squeezing his hand a little tighter.

He waited, listening until the scrabbling died away before starting again, more urgently this time.

'Have you got the key?'

'What? You want to open it?'

'Janey, have you got the key or not?'

'Okay, okay.'

She pulled a bunch of keys from the coat she had slung over a chair and held one out. Cal took it and moved to the door. At the sound of his approach, the scrabbling stopped, replaced by the rattle of the key in the lock. He opened the door just a crack at first, and peered out before letting it swing back on its hinges.

Outside, a small shed and a few items of garden furniture were silhouetted in the darkness. Cal waited before calling out.

'Frost? Frost! Come on, boy.'

There was no movement; the shadowy garden was as quiet as a graveyard. Cal, thinking he may have been mistaken, reached to pull the door shut, but not before a white flash appeared from the darkness and charged through the opening, leaping up onto the kitchen table. Cal jumped and Janey swore loudly. A cat, proud and tall, cast star bright yellow eyes over them.

'Frost!' cried Janey, running to him and stroking a hand down his back. 'I thought the Severals had finished you off.'

Two patches of bare skin glistened with blood where black nails had torn the fur from the Chattan. He shivered as Janey touched them, although he made no sound. He backed across the table and sat, watching her. Cal shut the door.

'He's hurt, Cal.'

'He'll be fine. I think if he needed help, he'd let you help him.'

Cal ruffled his fingers behind the cat's neck and Frost pushed his head against Cal's palm, purring loudly.

'Thanks, Frost,' said Cal gently. 'We'd have been in big trouble out there if it wasn't for you.'

The cat butted him playfully and then sat.

'Listen,' Cal continued, 'we're gonna need your help again. The Nephilim have captured Dad and the Baudouin.'

Frost watched him, unblinking.

'I need to get to *Podwitch* and find out what we have to do to stop all this.'

Frost lifted a front paw and began licking it. Cal glanced at Janey, who shrugged her shoulders. When the cat was convinced the paw was clean, he looked back at Cal and then hopped down from the table and skipped to the back door, lifting a paw to scratch at the wood. Cal opened it, letting the Chattan squeeze through before closing it again.

'What do we do now?' asked Janey.

'We wait,' said Cal.

*

As the kitchen clock marked the passing minutes, ushering them towards the unknown, an eerie quiet replaced the shouts in the street. The silence was even worse. Just as Cal thought he couldn't take any more, he heard a slight scrabbling at the back door.

Janey leapt up and unlocked the door, flinging it open. Peering out, she gasped.

'What's wrong?'

'You need to look at this.'

Cal crossed to the door.

Outside, shapes moved in the darkness, obscuring the garden furniture that had been visible before. But they weren't Severals, they were Chattan. Standing, sitting, lying. They watched the children without a sound.

'Blimey!' Janey muttered. 'There are loads of them.'

Something brushed against Cal's calf. He looked down.

'Twilight!' he cried, picking her up. She rubbed against him briefly and then pulled away, inspecting him for any sign of injury. 'I'm fine, I promise.'

She began purring loudly.

'It's good to see you,' Cal said, feeling his eyes brim with tears. 'But everything's gone wrong.'

Twilight jumped down, trotting over to Frost. The two Chattan nuzzled one another, exchanging a series of mews and whines. They were interrupted by the sounds of smashing glass and shouting, which echoed up the side of the house, coming from the street.

Cal followed Twilight and Frost as they padded back through the kitchen and into the living room. They both jumped lightly onto the windowsill and crouched, still as statues, focusing intently on the scene outside.

The calm had only been temporary. At the far end of the street, groups of people had gathered and were arguing. Some were fighting. There were two cars with smashed windows. A small fire was burning in a garden. The Severals skittered over the scene like ants.

'It's getting worse,' said Cal.

Frost jumped down and ran out of the room.

'Whatever's happening, we have to stop it.' He balled his fists with a new resolve, strengthened by Twilight's arrival. 'We must get to *Podwitch*, and fast.'

A mewing came from the kitchen and Twilight dashed out. Cal followed her and found the rest of the Chattan flooding in through the back door. They scampered into the hallway, either side of Cal's feet.

'Get your coat, Janey,' he said. 'I think we're leaving.'

'Mum's not gonna be very happy about this,' said Janey, watching them leap over the table, chairs and worktops.

'It can't be helped. Come on.'

Janey locked the back door and joined Cal in the hallway, where the Chattan had positioned themselves in rows.

'They're ready,' said Cal.

'Ready for what?' asked Janey.

She was trying to navigate her way between the cats when there was a loud shriek and one of them leapt up, hissing angrily.

'Sorry!'

'Come on,' Cal said, shaking his head.

Janey made it across the rest of the hallway, and they stood facing the front door. Behind them, the Chattan waited silently.

'Wait for my signal before we run,' said Cal. 'This is gonna be close.'

His head had started to throb with anticipation.

'Cal, I'm scared.' Janey's voice sounded lost in the darkness.

'Me too,' he replied, taking her hand in his.

He counted to three before yanking the door open.

Twilight and Frost were out first, streaking across the lawn and leaping the fence before Cal could blink. The children's legs were buffeted as the rest of the Chattan swarmed forward, a small sea of fur hurtling into the night.

TWENTY

Back To Podwitch

S ounds of battle hung in the air as Cal and Janey
watched solemnly from the doorway. The Chattan
fought wildly. They bit, clawed and slashed, pushing
steadily towards the top of the street, allowing the
children space to escape.

'Go!' cried Cal.

Janey darted ahead and he followed. They turned out
of the gate, away from the battle. At the end of the road,
they paused and glanced back.

Initially surprised, the Severals appeared afraid of the
cats, jostling to keep out of their way. But more continued
to swarm over rooftops, further swelling their numbers. It
wasn't long before they realised the odds were in their favour
and soon they were fighting back. Despite things turning
against them, the small Chattan continued fighting bravely.

A soft patter of paws came towards the children and

Twilight appeared from the shadows, jumping up onto Cal's shoulder in a single bound. He raised his hand and felt her sides heaving before they were off again.

The Severals' attack had been concentrated in just a few roads; in neighbouring streets, there was no sign of them. Nevertheless, Cal knew it wouldn't be long before they caught their scent. He scanned rooftops and alleyways for any sign of them as he ran.

They descended the steps leading to the canal quickly and raced along the towpath. Twilight leapt from Cal's shoulder and ran on ahead. She lifted her nose, smelling the air, her tail thrashing wildly. Light crept out through Mr Bentley's curtains as they crossed the gangplank onto *Podwitch*. Cal's hands were shaking so much he was unable to get the door key into the lock.

'Hurry,' Janey's voice pleaded. 'They're coming.'

Cal glanced back and saw a group of dark shapes approaching quickly. Despite the protective bubble surrounding them, he couldn't stand the thought of the Severals coming close to him again. He fumbled, the key jamming in the lock.

'Cal!' cried Janey.

He scrabbled, unable to dislodge the key. As Twilight mewed above him on the roof, Cal felt like screaming in frustration. At last, the key gave under his hand, sliding into the lock and turning quickly. He wrenched open the doors. Janey and Twilight entered before he descended the steps after them, pulling the doors shut as the first Severals ran into the wall of protection, beating their fists against it in fury.

*

'Okay, so now what?' asked Janey.

'I'm not sure,' said Cal.

He moved quickly to draw the curtains across the portholes. He wanted to ensure *Podwitch* remained as inconspicuous as possible. The protection would be too strong for the Severals, but it was Thorne he was worried about. He lit an oil lamp, keeping the wick low as Twilight paced the living room restlessly.

'Come on, Cal. Think. Didn't your dad say something about using a book?'

He stopped and looked at her.

'You're right. Wait a minute, where is it?'

Cal ran a hand along the bookshelf on the cabin wall.

'Got it,' he said, pulling down the thick leather hardback.

'What is it?' asked Janey.

'A book Charles Dickens gave Dad ages ago. I remember he said something about it telling you what you need to know. Funny, I didn't think about it at the time. I wonder what he meant.'

Cal flicked through the pages as he spoke. They smelt musty and some were discoloured and dog-eared.

'Maybe there are clues in the story?' suggested Janey.

'That's no good to us now. I've hardly got time to read through this. It's massive.'

He frowned and closed the book, taking a moment to inspect the cover in case he had missed something. But apart from the title and author's name, there was nothing.

'Cal,' said Janey.

'What?' he answered, not looking at her.

'I think the Pod's trying to tell you something.'

Cal stopped and put a hand to the Pod. It was warm, only just, but warm nevertheless. He looked down and saw a faint blue glow deep inside it. Jeb had been right; it was working again. He put down the book, took his other hand and held it between his fingers, examining it.

'Hey, the light's fading,' said Janey.

Sure enough, the Pod was grey once more, and rapidly cooling in Cal's fingers. 'It's the book,' he said, reaching for it.

When he picked up the book, the light and warmth returned to the Pod. It was fainter than he had seen it before, but definitely reacting.

'What does it mean?' asked Janey, leaning forward.

'*The Pickwick Papers*,' Cal read, holding the book up in front of him. 'By Charles Dickens.'

He shifted his position and as he did so, the faint blue light splashed across the front cover. Cal stopped and stared. Then he moved the Pod over the book, letting the light hover over it. He blinked and looked again. The title of the book had changed.

Now it simply said:

POD GUIDE

Cal opened the cover. The printed chapter index that had previously been inside was blank. Instead, written in the same typeface were the words:

To gain advantage over the Nephilim, seek the Podmap and meet with the Blue Plaque Network.

'Will they be able to help me rescue Dad?' Cal asked.

It felt weird, speaking to a book. But then the book seemed to be writing itself in front of him. Nothing happened so Cal repeated the question. Again nothing.

'Try turning the page, like you're reading it,' said Janey, who was now kneeling next to him.

Cal turned the page.

'Will the Blue Plaque Network be able to help me rescue Dad?' he repeated.

More words materialised in front of him:

They can advise you in ways of advantage. Their knowledge is great.

'What does Thorne want?' asked Cal, turning the next page.

My purpose is to advise action, not explain motive...

Cal turned the page patiently.

'There must be something else you can tell me,' he demanded.

But the book simply repeated its first instruction:

To gain advantage over the Nephilim, seek the Podmap and meet with the Blue Plaque Network.

He flipped the page again and saw the same phrase repeated. Flicking through the rest of the book, he saw it was the same on all the remaining pages. He slammed it shut and let go of the Pod, making his way through to Jeb's room. He scrabbled under the bed, emerging after several minutes with the folded map in his hand.

'Got it,' he said, running back along the corridor and holding it up for Janey to see.

Now, more than ever, he needed Charles Dickens. It *had* to work. Sensing his nerves, Twilight appeared on the arm of the chair and nuzzled him. Cal spread the map over the low table and reached for the Pod. It was so small; how could it possibly contain enough power to defeat what they were up against? What if it remained lifeless? As he pondered, he felt it grow warm under his fingers. His heart surged and he knew, before pulling it out, that the blue Podlight would be glowing once more.

Janey stared as Cal lifted the chain over his head and dangled the Pod over the map, waiting. Seconds ticked by, but it wasn't long before the map came to life in front of their eyes, the ink becoming bold where before it had been faint. There were no clouds this time. The view was clear, and the city shimmered with lights and movement.

'It's alive again,' whispered Janey.

Cal held his breath and lowered the Pod slowly. Sure enough, the city came towards them. He lowered it again until London's street names became visible, holding his hand steady, sweat lining his brow. He hoped the Pod was at the correct height and waited for it to move, barely breathing. Seconds passed relentlessly, measured by the steady tick of the kitchen clock.

Cal's arm had started to ache when he felt a slight movement. His hand remained perfectly still as the Pod began to swing, sending the map whirling in broad circles. The blue plaques darted across the surface of the paper. Streets and buildings moved in a blur and Janey put her hands to the side of her head, trying to steady herself before it began to slow down. Slower and slower the map moved until finally it came to a standstill and the beam of light connected the Pod with a blue disc at its centre. Cal leaned forward to read it:

221b Baker Street, Sherlock Holmes, Consulting Detective 1881-1904

'Sherlock Holmes?' said Cal, frowning. 'Wait a minute, that can't be right. There must be a mistake.'

He lifted the Pod up and instantly they were miles above the city once more. At the same time, the blue light faded and the Pod became dull and grey. When Cal lowered it again, it remained lifeless.

'You m... mean... are you trying to tell me that we're g... gonna go...' Janey stammered.

'To see Sherlock Holmes? Yeah, I guess so, but I don't get it. Sherlock Holmes wasn't a real person. He was just a character in stories.' Cal put the Pod back around his neck and folded the map up, sliding it inside his coat. 'I didn't even know he had a blue plaque. I suppose if there's one with his name on it, then there must be something to it. After everything we've seen and heard in the last few days, it wouldn't be that crazy, would it?'

'I can't believe it,' was all Janey could say.

'I guess we'll have to go to Baker Street and see what happens,' said Cal. 'Somebody will be there who can help us, even if it isn't Sherlock Holmes.' He glanced across at the kitchen clock. 'Right, it's nearly eight o'clock. We can only access the blue plaque after midnight. We'll set off from here in plenty of time in case there are any problems. There's lots we need to talk about with Twilight on the way.'

Janey reached out a hand to stroke the black and white Chattan. Twilight regarded her coolly before moving to Cal's lap and curling into a tight ball.

'I'm going to try and get some rest,' said Cal.

'Me too,' said Janey. 'Though there's too much going on for me to relax. Do you seriously think you'll be able to sle…?'

A snore stopped her and she glanced at Cal, who was fast asleep already, his head lolling back against the chair. She watched him for a moment, before reaching into her coat pocket. She rummaged inside and pulled out her mobile phone.

'A text to Mum won't hurt,' she said, her fingers already skimming over the keypad. 'Just so she knows I'm safe.'

*

A harsh beep woke Cal, and as his eyes adjusted, he strained his ears to identify the source. The gentle hiss of the oil lamp accompanied his confusion. Its light seemed more dirty than normal, staining the whitewashed walls yellow. The coal stove at the heart of the narrowboat remained dark and empty. The air was cold. It hurt when he breathed. Twilight was on her feet at the front doors, fur standing on end and back arched, a low whine coming from her mouth. Janey's mobile lay on the arm of her chair, its screen glowing brightly as it confirmed delivery of her earlier text message.

Cal jumped up, sleep forgotten, senses alert. He grabbed the phone, searching for the button to switch it off. The Pod was icy against his skin and his hand reached for it as its blue light spilled into the room. Janey groaned in her sleep and turned in the chair.

Without another thought, Cal went to the front doors and pulled back the bolts, tucking the Pod inside his jumper and zipping up his coat, ensuring it couldn't be seen. Twilight sprang onto his shoulder and he found himself glad for her warmth. He pulled the doors open and moved up the steps, keeping his eyes focused on the deck and closing the doors behind him, keen to let Janey avoid what was to follow. He couldn't feel angry with her. He probably wouldn't have made it this far without her, but he cursed silently under his breath at how easily they had surrendered their place of sanctuary.

Cal suspected what he would find before he stepped out, but nothing could prepare him for the sight that met his eyes on that cold December night.

Instead of drifting off as usual, the large numbers of Severals that had followed them earlier in the evening had multiplied. Not one surface outside the protection of the narrowboat could be seen, so covered were they in dark, throbbing shapes. It was as though all light had been sucked from the world, leaving *Podwitch* at its cold and lifeless centre. Gone were the towpath and the steep brick wall leading to the street above. Gone were the neighbouring narrowboats. Gone was the water of the canal, and gone was the sound of the city.

The Severals sniffed eagerly as he emerged. Some lunged forward at him. Cal winced, half expecting them to reach through the barrier easily. But it held firm and they groaned in frustration. The protection may have weakened but *Podwitch* was still safe. He shivered and raised a hand to Twilight. Together they faced the darkness all around.

Podwitch, the secret and protected home of the Aldhelm, was under siege.

TWENTY-ONE

A Nephilim's Challenge

The Severals parted, revealing a glimpse of the towpath behind. A figure appeared in the gap, striding through it slowly, coming to a halt at the edge of the protective bubble. Cal saw Thorne's talons as he lit his cigarette and dropped the match.

'So we meet again, young Wainwright,' whispered the Nephilim. 'Thank your little friend for the tip-off.'

'She didn't know,' Cal replied.

Hissing laughter eased from Thorne's mouth.

'I'm not afraid of you,' Cal said, his voice shaking. 'I know what you are.'

A chorus of excited snorts emanated from the Severals.

'What have you done with my dad?' he asked.

'The Aldhelm is in a place where he can do no more damage. He and his French friend have provided stubborn opposition for too long. Their time is done.'

'Where are they?'

Thorne's smile was chilling.

'You will find out soon enough,' he whispered. 'But let's just say, neither of them put up much of a fight. And now, future Aldhelm, as you see, there is no use in trying to hide. Perhaps you would like to invite me on board for a conversation. It is so… chilly out here.'

'You'll never step foot on *Podwitch*.'

Thorne took a long drag on his cigarette before continuing.

'A pity… but no less than expected. It is a problem that your father and the Baudouin were captured without their Pods.'

He spat the final word as though it tasted unpleasant.

'Then what's the point in keeping them captive?' Cal asked. 'It's not them you want, is it? It's the Pods. It's the Podmagic you need to control.'

Thorne grimaced. 'Precisely. And that, Wainwright, is where you fit in. You see, as laughable as it seems, *I* need *your* help.'

'You have got to be joking!' yelled Janey, appearing behind Cal. She immediately clamped a hand to her mouth.

The Nephilim's eyes flicked to her. 'I don't recall talking to you,' he said. His voice was the sound of a boat's hull grinding across sharpened rocks.

'You need my help?' asked Cal, keen to draw Thorne's attention from his friend.

'I need the Aldhelm's Pod,' Thorne whispered.

'And why should I help you?'

'Because it's worth the life of your father and that walking French fossil.'

'You mean…'

'If the Pods are in your possession or you know where to find them, and you don't do as I ask, the Pod Guardians will die.'

Twilight's claws dug into Cal's shoulder.

'And what if I don't know where they are?' he answered, his voice shaking.

'THEN YOU HAD BETTER FIND THEM QUICKLY,' screeched the Nephilim.

The Severals shrank back and the children threw their hands to their ears. Thorne stared at them from behind his sunglasses and continued, his voice quiet again.

'You have until the stroke of midnight tomorrow. If I don't have the Pods in my possession by then, you will become the new Aldhelm as your father ceases to exist.'

Cal frowned. 'But that means you'll die too.'

'Ah, you've been doing your homework.' Thorne smiled. 'Whether I live or die is of no consequence. Another Nephilim will replace me and the two of you will soon become acquainted. You see, the great weakness of the Pod Guardians is that they form close friendships with family and friends and become compromised when making important decisions. We Nephilim do not allow ourselves to indulge in such sentiment.'

He smiled and took another long drag on his cigarette.

'Where should I meet you?' Cal asked quietly.

'Cal, you can't!' cried Janey.

He ignored her, his mouth dry. 'Where?' he repeated.

'On Parliament Hill, where you met the Baudouin. It is a fitting stage for the occasion, and a reminder that the balance of power has shifted,' whispered Thorne.

Cal nodded.

'So, future Aldhelm, let's see if you have promise… without your precious father to help you.'

The Nephilim shot him one last smile and turned away. His laughter hung in the air long after the Severals had closed ranks behind him.

*

Cal paced up and down the cabin. It was two minutes before midnight and Twilight sat calmly in a chair watching him. Janey peered nervously through a porthole.

'They're still out there,' she said, dropping the curtain back in place. 'Cal, you haven't spoken for half an hour. Why don't you sit down?'

'Can't… got to think,' he mumbled.

All he could think of was talking to Twilight; she'd be able to help. When midnight finally arrived, Cal spun around.

'What should I do, Twilight? You heard Thorne. He's gonna kill Dad and Jean unless we give him the Pods.'

Twilight waited before answering in her silky drawl.

'You should listen to your friend here. If you don't stop pacing up and down this room, I'll go mad.'

Cal stopped and stared at her. 'I'm serious,' he said.

'And so am I. You must calm down. This is no time for hysterics.'

Whether it was the Chattan's words, the tone of her voice, or her stare, Cal wasn't sure, but he dropped into the empty chair without complaint.

'Okay, what are we gonna do?' he said.

'We can't give the Pods to Thorne,' said Janey. 'Whatever he said, we can't do it.'

'On that we agree,' said Twilight.

'But what choice do we have? He's going to kill them!' replied Cal.

'If Jeb and Legard valued their lives more than the Pods, they would have given them up,' said Twilight, sitting up. 'Think about it, Cal. By passing them to you, they have forfeited their right to life.'

'Just like that? Without a fight?'

'It's their responsibility, Cal. They are Guardians of the Pods, which means ensuring they aren't destroyed or end up in the wrong hands. If you let Thorne seize them, you'll undo centuries of sacrifice.'

'What happens if Thorne gets hold of them?' asked Janey.

'Who knows?' replied the Chattan. 'Untold power would be placed in the hands of a ruthless agent of the Mist, who would stop at nothing to use it against other Guardians the world over. No, the Pods cannot be given to the Nephilim. Ever.'

'There must be something we can do,' Cal said.

'There's always something that can be done.'

Cal sat forward. 'What?'

'What was it Jeb told you to do when he handed over the Pod? What were you going to do before Thorne showed up?'

'He told me to consult the Podmap, which I did. You saw me.'

'So what's stopping you consulting with the Blue Plaque Network?' replied Twilight coolly.

'What the hell are you talking about, Twilight?' cried Cal. His voice shook with sudden emotion. 'We can't leave *Podwitch*. You've seen all the Severals out there. The Pod is too weak. We wouldn't stand a chance.'

'Sit down, Cal!' bellowed Twilight in a voice far too powerful for her small body. Janey jumped out of her skin and the Chattan stood up, her fur standing on end. 'This is no way for the future Aldhelm to behave. You'll treat me with respect or risk losing me altogether. My only interest is the well-being of the Pod and the preservation of your father. I have no time for childish tantrums!'

Cal sat slowly in his chair, avoiding eye contact with the Chattan. Twilight continued staring at him. When she spoke, her voice was velvet once more.

'I'm sorry, Cal. Chattan are quick in temper, and I should make allowances for the pressure you're under. But I'm trying to help and if we're to work together, you must listen to me.'

'I'm the one who should be sorry,' Cal replied quietly.

'I shouldn't have shouted. I guess I'm just pretty freaked out by everything.'

'These apologies are very nice and all that, you two,' interrupted Janey, 'but if we don't stop talking soon and actually do something, it's going to be tomorrow night before we know it and it'll all be over anyway.'

Twilight stared at her without blinking and Janey fell silent.

'Where was I?' said the Chattan. 'Ah yes, the Plaque Network. You're right, Cal. For us to venture outside *Podwitch* would be unthinkable. I can protect you against perhaps three or four Severals, but any more than that and we wouldn't stand a chance. As for the Nephilim, as much as I'd love to take him on, I would be no match for him.'

'So how do we get to Baker Street?' asked Cal, confused.

'For that, you must consult the *Pod Guide*,' Twilight said gently.

'Of course!' said Cal. With Thorne's appearance, he had forgotten about the book. He picked it up and opened it, holding the Pod over it so that the blue light fell across its pages.

'How can we travel to Baker Street and avoid Thorne and the Severals?' he asked.

As the words appeared in front of him, he swallowed.

'What is it, Cal? What's wrong?' asked Janey.

Cal glanced up at his friend.

'It says there's only one way. And that's through the Labyrinth.'

TWENTY-TWO

Descent

———————

'What the hell is the Labyrinth?' asked Janey, interrupting the silence.

'It's somewhere we don't want to go,' replied Cal.

'Believe me,' Twilight said quietly, 'I've no desire to return to that place and would do anything to avoid it. I travelled there with your father many years ago. We were lucky to escape with our lives.'

'But if the *Pod Guide* says it's the only way, we may have no choice.'

'I'm not sure I like the sound of this,' said Janey. 'Maybe we should see if the Severals are still outside. I'd rather risk them.'

'We should get ready to go,' Cal said, ignoring her. 'Are you both coming?'

'Of course,' answered Twilight.

Cal looked at Janey.

'Okay, count me in, but Mum's gonna go mad,' she muttered.

'Cal,' said Twilight, 'you need to see if you can open the gateway. Remember, Jeb uses a Podhex to seal it.'

'How am I supposed to know what it is? He never told me what word he uses.'

'You must use your instinct,' said Twilight. 'And the Pod can help you.'

Cal moved the coffee table and crouched over the rug, taking a corner of it in his fingers. He could sense Janey and Twilight watching him.

'It's beneath the boat?' he heard Janey whisper.

Cal shifted position, moving onto his knees. With the rug in one hand and the Pod in the other, he closed his eyes. He tried to think of words and phrases that would be significant to Jeb, something that nobody else would know. But nothing came to him; his mind was too overloaded with information and emotion. He opened his eyes and sighed loudly.

'Try and relax,' said Twilight calmly. 'Take your time.'

He took a deep breath and loosened his shoulders, emptying his head of everything. Time was one thing he didn't have. Gripping the corner of the rug tightly, focusing on the feel of it in his hand, Cal waited for the command to come to him. He realised that he was concentrating so hard that he'd stopped breathing. He continued to hold his breath, just in case the very act itself would break his concentration. Cal began to think he would never stand a chance of uncovering the password. Numbers, dates, times and other pieces of information tumbled through his mind, until he thought his chest might burst.

It was then that he glanced up, his eyes coming to rest on the photo of his mum. Out of nowhere, it came to him. He felt the Pod grow warm beneath his fingers as though encouraging him, and suddenly he was certain of it. Without opening his eyes, he spoke his mum's name under his breath, waiting for a second before whipping the rug away. Janey gasped. Cal looked at the trapdoor and saw its golden handle glinting in the lamplight. He shot a glance at Twilight.

'Well done,' she said warmly.

'What was it?' asked Janey. 'The word, I mean.'

Cal was about to answer her, when he hesitated.

'I don't think I'm supposed to tell,' he said. 'Sorry.'

Cal had a profound sense that life was going to be full of information he could never share and things he wished he could say but could never speak of.

'I guess we should pack anything we think we'll need,' he said, turning to the gateway. 'I'll carry it in my rucksack.'

'You should take the *Pod Guide*, Cal,' said Twilight. 'You never know what might be in there that could help.'

'Good idea,' he said.

He emptied out the contents of his rucksack and Janey brought over an armful of bread, cheese, ham, tomatoes and two bottles of water. They made up a flask of hot chocolate on Twilight's advice.

'It can get pretty chilly down there,' she said.

When everything was packed, Cal handed a torch to Janey.

'You'll need this.'

'What about you?'

'The Podlight will show me the way. This is just in case we get split up. If we do, stay where you are until I can find you. Try finding your way without me and the Pod, and you could be lost forever.'

Janey gulped and flicked the torch.

'Are the batteries strong enough?' she asked, shining the beam into Cal's eyes.

'They're fine,' he said. 'Look, we're not going to get split up, it's just in case. Okay?'

She nodded, gripping the torch with both hands. Cal glanced out of a porthole. The Severals hovered, turning their blind eyes from side to side and sniffing the air.

'Right,' he said, turning back. 'I'll go first, with Twilight.'

The Chattan hopped into the open rucksack, poking her head out of the top. Janey lifted the bag carefully, passing the straps over Cal's arms until it was secure against his back.

'How's that, Twilight?' he asked, turning his head.

'Apart from the general lack of comfort and dignity, it's acceptable,' she grumbled.

'I'll get to the bottom as quickly as possible.'

'Safety is more important than speed, Cal. There's a shelf cut into the rock halfway down. It's a good place to stop and rest.'

'How long will it take us to get there?'

'It's best not to think of time. Just focus on conserving your energy.'

The children looked at one another. Just how deep was this Labyrinth?

Cal leaned forward and pulled on the golden handle, and the trapdoor swung open. A sharp wind rose out of the shaft, causing the curtains to sway and the saucepans to clang together on the kitchen wall. It was followed by a dank, unpleasant odour that flooded the cabin. Cal shivered as a sense of dread seemed to reach up from the Labyrinth and wrap a hand around him, pulling him towards the shaft when all he really wanted to do was to get as far from it as possible. He heard a mewing sound from Twilight, who had ducked low in the rucksack. If Janey's grip on the torch had been tight before, she was now in danger of crushing it completely. Her knuckles were white.

'Are you absolutely sure about this, Cal?' she asked.

Glancing around his home, Cal realised all the safety and comfort it had offered up to now had been snuffed out, leaving him feeling alone and scared. He looked at his mum's photo. Some of the pain of her disappearance returned to him. Her smile had always been able to lift him in dark moments.

'I'm afraid,' was all he could respond.

For a moment, everything threatened to collapse in on him and he grasped the Pod tighter than he ever had before, willing it to protect him.

'Cal, we have to go.' Twilight's voice was as soft as sunlight, as strong as steel. 'Jeb's life is in danger,' she continued. 'You are the Aldhelm now, at least until we can find him. The fate of the world is your responsibility, as it was his, and your grandmother's before him. There is no time for fear. We *must* leave immediately.'

Cal peered at the opening in the cabin floor and swallowed.

'This is just the beginning, isn't it, Twilight?' he said.

The Chattan didn't respond, but nuzzled him gently. He steadied his breathing and lowered himself to sit on the floor with his legs hanging down into the shaft. After a last look around the cabin, he placed his feet on the top rung and took the upright struts in his hands. The metal was icy cold and he gasped as the chill passed quickly up his arms. Then he was off, descending slowly, letting each foot find the next rung before moving his hands to follow.

The walls were closer than they had looked from above, so close in fact that Cal was barely a few inches from them on any side. He pictured the canal water just the other side of them and fought to keep himself calm. It would do them no good to start panicking so close to the top. Besides, it wasn't as though the shaft literally passed through the canal; it was here but not here, directly connected to *Podwitch* wherever she was and not the physical space beneath her. When his feet reached the tenth rung, he stopped.

'Ready?' he called up.

'As I'll ever be,' replied Janey.

She lowered herself into the gap.

'Cal,' Twilight's voice was close to his ear. 'Janey's going to have to close the gateway.'

'What?'

'In order for the Pod to work in the Labyrinth, the gateway must be sealed. Not closing it would leave a doorway into the world of men, through which anything could climb or crawl.'

'But we know the Labyrinth has already been breached. What difference does it make?'

'It's the way of things. The Pod won't work down here unless the specific gateway through which it enters is closed, no matter what others are open.'

Cal's mind raced. The thought of shutting themselves into the shaft was not a pleasant one. Keeping the comforting glow of the oil lamp in sight above him was the only way he thought he could manage the descent.

'What's going on down there?' came Janey's voice. 'If this is as fast as we're gonna go, we'll never get to the bottom!'

Cal braced himself and spoke firmly.

'Janey, you're going to have to close the trapdoor.'

There was a pause.

'You are having a laugh!'

'Listen to me, it's the only way the Pod will work. If you don't, then it won't show us the way.'

'I'm not climbing down this ladder in the pitch black, Cal. No way.'

'There'll be more light if we close it than if we don't. I know you don't want to, neither do I, but we have to trust the Pod. If not, we're gonna be lost down here without it, and that'll be a lot worse, right?'

There was silence and Cal's hands grew numb as the

cold metal bit into his fingers. He heard Janey moving and looked up to see her climbing back up the ladder, before a mighty thud resonated around the shaft. At the same time, it was plunged into darkness so thick he could no longer see his hands just inches in front of him.

'There you go!' came Janey's voice. 'Now where is the bloody light?'

Cal gripped the ladder tightly and fought the rising panic. Why wasn't it working? He was about to ask Janey to open the trapdoor again, when Podlight suddenly flooded the shaft, coating it in an eerie blue glow.

'Thank God for that!' called Janey.

Cal exhaled through gritted teeth. Invigorated, he started moving again, one rung at a time, leaving *Podwitch* and the world above them.

Once he'd got used to the distance between rungs, Cal found a rhythm in his movements and increased his speed, Janey following him. Their shoes scraped dully on the metal rungs, stifled by the close proximity of the walls. He quickly lost any sense of feeling in his hands as the metal gnawed at them. Soon, numbness turned to aching pain, and the only way to avoid it was by stopping every few rungs to lift first one hand and then the other, flexing his fingers.

The air in the shaft was thick and stale, and breathing became harder the further they went down. Cal found the best way to cope was to take short, regular breaths and called up to Janey, advising her to do the same. Their clothes were soon covered in a fine layer of dampness, and moisture coated their hair, running down the backs of their necks.

Like a predator, waiting just beyond the blue light, darkness seemed poised for an opportunity to snatch them from the ladder.

At one point, Cal nearly lost his grip. His head was spinning so much he had to rest it against the ladder until the dizziness had passed. From that moment on, he kept his eyes forward, watching his hands, occasionally looking up to ensure Janey was still close.

All sense of time disappeared in the shaft, and after what felt like a day, Twilight spoke for the first time since the gateway had been closed.

'The rock ledge is coming up in nine rungs. You'll need to reach out with your foot to find it.'

Cal counted the rungs carefully. At the ninth, he paused. His body had become so used to the motion of descending that it felt strange to stop. He took a moment to steady himself and reached out a foot to the left. Pins and needles shot up his leg. He groaned and drew his foot back, waiting for the blood to circulate. When his leg felt normal, he reached out again. This time, it connected with the ledge. Glancing across, he could see it bathed in blue, cut about five feet into the wall, a sort of squared-off cave in the side of the shaft. He put his weight on his left foot, gradually transferring it from his right, and then let go of the ladder, moving across the gap into the opening.

'I'm here, I've done it!' he called up.

Cal placed his backpack on the floor and Twilight

hopped out, stretching and arching her back. He held the Pod up so Janey could see the ledge. She crossed the gap easily and soon they were both shaking their limbs to gain some feeling back.

'Let's have some hot chocolate and a rest before we get going again,' Cal said.

He pulled out the flask, poured steaming liquid into a mug and handed it to Janey. Cal offered Twilight a bowl of water, then he and Janey nibbled on some bread and cheese.

'How many rungs do you reckon that was?' asked Janey.

'No idea,' said Cal.

'We're exactly halfway down,' answered Twilight. 'It's best not to think about how many you've climbed.'

'Easy for you to say,' grumbled Janey, rubbing her calf.

Cal waited for Twilight's response, but none came. She stared coolly at Janey. It must have turned one o'clock; she had been silenced by the curse.

The realisation left Cal feeling lonely and he took a moment to consider their situation. Here they were, hundreds of feet underneath London in a tiny, damp shaft, sitting on a ledge bathed in magical blue light from a Pod that had something to do with protecting the world. Not to mention what might be waiting for them if they ever got to the bottom of the ladder. The whole thing was so bizarre he had the sudden notion he might wake up on *Podwitch*, safe and snug in his bed a week ago, to find it had all been a dream. But he knew, as crazy as it was, that this was no dream. He knew Jeb and Monsieur Legard were in real danger and that he, Janey and Twilight were their only hope. The thought spurred him on and he jumped up.

'Come on, let's get going.'

With Twilight secured in the backpack, they began the final descent. The aching throb soon returned in their hands, and their legs seemed stiffer than before. The further they went, the colder and more damp the shaft became. Vapour poured from their mouths as they breathed.

After some time, Cal paused. The thought of more climbing was becoming too much and he leaned forward, resting against the ladder.

'What's going on? You okay?' called Janey.

'I'm not sure I can move.'

There was a pause.

'Well, we can't stay here, can we? Come on, Cal, this is no time to quit. Sort yourself out!'

Cal wished Twilight was able to speak to him and offer comfort, but none came. Instead, he heard her purring and felt her nuzzle the back of his neck. It was enough and he pulled his head back, taking a firm grip on the ladder. He flexed his legs and started off again.

'It's okay, Janey,' he called up. 'I'm okay.'

'Thank God for that. Now let's try and get off this bloody ladder!'

Cal moved more quickly now, pushing the pain in his hands to the back of his mind. Behind him, Twilight purred in encouragement, and above, Janey was pushing him faster with the speed of her descent. He was so focused on the rhythm of his movement that when his foot didn't meet the expected next rung, his whole body jolted with the effort of not letting himself fall. He fumbled for the rungs, clinging desperately to the ladder.

'Stop, Janey, wait!' he called.

Cal took a moment to ensure he was under control and then carefully adjusted his weight, pointing his toe downwards. What if the ladder was broken? He tried not to panic and stretched his foot lower. Just as he was about to give up, his toe met with something soft. Cal lowered the Pod until he could see the bottom rung, suspended several feet above a bed of sand. They had finally made it. He stepped down off the ladder, legs shaking.

'I'm at the bottom!' he called up.

Janey descended the last few rungs quickly and jumped down onto the sand.

'Thank God for that,' she said, breathing heavily. 'I thought it was never going to end.'

Cal held the Pod above his head, staring upwards. The shaft had ended high above, opening out into a large cave through which the ladder was suspended, eventually coming to within two feet of the sandy floor on which they now found themselves standing.

'There must be a tunnel or something that leads out of here, right, Twilight?' Cal asked.

The Chattan purred in encouragement behind him.

'You ready, Janey?'

'No point in waiting,' she replied.

As they headed across the cavern floor, Cal glanced back. The ladder had already been swallowed by the darkness.

TWENTY-THREE

Tunnels And Tumbles

———

I t took several minutes to reach the cavern's perimeter. They followed the rock wall, tracing their hands across its jagged surface until they reached two openings, standing next to each other like gaping mouths. Janey grabbed Cal's fingers tightly. Without speaking, the children approached the one to the right. The Podlight faded quickly.

'What's going on?' asked Janey.

'Wrong way,' answered Cal. 'It must be the other tunnel.'

He stepped towards the left-hand opening and the Pod blazed. Once inside, they moved swiftly, the feeling returning to their legs after the long descent.

The passage was wide enough for them to walk side by side, and just high enough to stand upright. The rock walls were oddly smooth, not natural at all. Strange symbols covered their surface, etched in muted colours. Cal couldn't make them out, but some looked like words written in a strange language, others like images of unrecognisable animals. On seeing them, Twilight mewed nervously and ducked down inside the rucksack.

The passageway led them into another cavern containing two more openings, one in the left-hand wall and one to the right. They tried the one to the left and the Podlight stayed strong.

This tunnel looked more natural, with walls of jagged rock that threatened to snag clothes and skin. It was lower than the previous passage, though, and it wasn't long before they were forced to bend over almost double as the angle of the roof came closer to the ground, making the going awkward and slow.

After ten minutes, they came to a knee-high lip of rock jutting up from the floor. Cal held the Pod out over the ridge and saw it drop away into vast darkness. Driven into the edge at his feet were two rusted metal stakes and attached to these was a rope ladder.

'What do you reckon?' he whispered.

'Well, it must lead somewhere, and the Pod seems to think it's right,' Janey replied. She wiped a hand over her face, where it left a trail of grime and sand.

A sudden noise came from the tunnel behind them, muffled and distant.

'What the hell was that?' said Janey in a loud whisper.

'It sounded like shouting,' replied Cal, 'but let's not wait around to find out.'

He swung himself over the edge and onto the rope ladder. It swayed beneath him but felt solid enough to take their combined weight.

'Come on!' he whispered.

Cal called out a rhythm by counting to ten and back as loudly as he dared, allowing them to move together and descend evenly, preventing the ladder from swinging too much. Although their arms and legs throbbed with the earlier climb, they moved quickly, fuelled by fear. It took no more than five minutes to reach the rock floor.

They were standing in what looked like a long, deep trench, which stretched away in either direction. Facing them were four openings, each a different shape and size. The blue light faded as they approached the first two tunnels but glowed encouragingly at the third.

'This way,' whispered Cal.

Just inside, the ground beneath their feet angled steeply away from them, heading further downward. Treading carefully, they fought to keep their balance on the damp rock, each putting a bracing hand to the sides of the tunnel for extra support.

'Are you sure this is right?' panted Janey. 'It looks impossible.'

'As long as the Pod tells us it is,' answered Cal, scrabbling for something to grasp onto.

Despite the chill, sweat was pouring from his forehead, running into his eyes. Without thinking, he took his hand from the wall to wipe them. It was then that he lost his footing.

Turning his body to avoid falling back onto Twilight, Cal heard Janey cry out as he slid downward, feet first on his front. He saw her face framed in the darkness, looking at him in terror. Then she was gone.

Cal reached out to grab something, but his skin grazed the rock painfully and he quickly pulled his hand back to his body. The Podlight thrashed about the walls and roof of the tunnel as shale rattled around him and he was buffeted from side to side like a pinball.

He cried out when the rock floor dropped away suddenly, and he was suspended in air for a few brief seconds, before falling with a splash into freezing water. Thrashing his arms and legs, Cal managed to lift his head above the surface and push himself onto his feet. Gulping deep breaths of air, he eased his arms out of the rucksack and unzipped it. But Twilight was not there. He delved into the water with his free hand, holding the Pod above him to see more clearly.

'Twilight, where are you?' he cried, splashing desperately for a sign of her. The ripples of his frantic search ran gently away from him, before being replaced by a surface as smooth as glass. Nothing. The Chattan was nowhere to be seen.

Janey was calling from the tunnel mouth, her voice echoing around the vast cavern. Cal waded to the opening and tried hauling himself up to it, but it was a metre above the line of the water and he didn't have the strength. He slid back awkwardly.

'Janey!' he shouted up. 'I can hear you, I'm okay! I need you to use the torch to find Twilight. I think she's lost somewhere in the tunnel. She might be hurt.'

Breathing hard and dripping with icy water, he turned and saw he was in a cave so large that the Podlight couldn't reach the ceiling or walls in any direction. Beneath his feet the floor was soft, sandy and submerged under water, which reached his waist and stretched out of sight. His eyes picked out something in the freezing darkness. An orange glow, twitching and flickering in the distance. He shivered.

'I don't even know if we're travelling in the right direction,' he muttered. 'What if the changes in the Podlight are random? If we were above ground, we'd have been at Baker Street ages ago.'

A shriek, followed by the sound of loose shale falling, preceded Janey's tumble from the cave opening. She dropped into the water and began thrashing about like a demented octopus. Cal rushed forward to help her up.

'Bloody hell!' she exclaimed, spitting out a mouthful of murky liquid.

She started pummelling her fists against Cal's chest and kicking out at him under the water.

'You pig! I can't believe you left me up there. You idiot! Why, Cal, why?'

Her cries reverberated about the cavern, sounding like a thousand banshees.

'Stop it, Janey, stop it! It's okay.'

At his words, her punches weakened and she collapsed against him, sobbing. Cal held her close and gradually she fell silent. When she was calm, she pulled away, wiping her eyes, speaking as if her outburst hadn't happened.

'I couldn't see Twilight anywhere. Are you sure she's not down here?' she said.

'Yes, and there's no way we can get back up now.'

'Maybe she'll find us on her own. Animals are clever like that.'

'Maybe,' Cal said glumly. 'Where's the torch?'

'I dropped it when I fell, and it smashed. I think it's broken.'

'It doesn't matter. We've got the Podlight and that's the last time we get split up,' said Cal.

'Promise?'

'Yeah, promise.'

Stones pattered down from the opening, pattering into the water like raindrops.

'Twilight?' called Cal, wading forward. 'Twilight, is that you?'

A laugh, distant and harsh, echoed towards him, followed by the same angry voices they had heard earlier.

'Let's get moving,' he said, backing towards Janey.

'What about Twilight?'

'She's gone.' Saying the words made him feel sick. 'Come on.'

They set off, sloshing slowly forward, sodden and cold.

'The Pod's taking us closer to that light,' whispered Janey after some time.

Cal didn't answer. When he'd tried to skirt around

the orange glow he'd glimpsed earlier, the Pod had faded; it wanted them to head directly for it.

It was some time before they were able to make out its source; a campfire, crackling at the centre of a small bank of sand that rose out of the water. Either side of the flames, two Y-shaped sticks had been driven into the sand. There was no sign of life. Cal and Janey approached cautiously.

'What do you reckon?' asked Janey.

'Someone must have made this fire. I think we should keep going.'

'But it looks so good, and it would be great to warm up, just for five minutes. I'm frozen and there's no one around.'

'We should really keep moving,' said Cal, eyeing the cheerful flames. He heard a clicking sound and realised it was his teeth chattering. 'Getting warm does sound great, though. But we can't be long.'

He tucked the Pod inside his jacket and the glow from the fire became the only light in an ocean of darkness. They stepped up from the shallows onto the soft sand, whipped off their shoes and socks and sat with their feet close to the flames, warming them through.

'That feels sooo good,' whispered Janey.

As they snuggled close to one another, Janey poured them some hot chocolate. They sipped the warm, sweet liquid, trying to draw comfort from the fire.

'Twilight…' Cal whispered. He shook his head.

'Wait a minute,' said Janey suddenly. 'Couldn't the *Pod Guide* tell you where she is?'

'Of course!' exclaimed Cal. He reached for his rucksack and felt inside. His heart stopped. 'It's gone,' he said quietly. 'It must have fallen out when I slipped. Just when things couldn't get any worse, I've lost that too.'

Neither of them said anything for some time. The crackle of the flames did its best to cheer them.

'This Labyrinth is creepy,' said Janey eventually. 'How far do you reckon we've come?'

'I've got no idea.' Cal didn't feel like talking.

'To think this place exists beneath London,' persisted Janey. 'It's really freaky. Where are the Tube trains and the sewers?'

Cal knew she was trying to distract him.

'I don't think we're actually under London,' he replied. 'It's like we're in a completely different place altogether. You can enter and leave from London, or anywhere else for that matter, as long as you know where the gateways are and how to open them. Twilight could explain it better than me...'

At the mention of the Chattan's name, he fell quiet. His throat tightened and he took a sip of chocolate. Janey waited before speaking.

'But we climbed down that shaft under the boat,' she said.

'Yeah, but the shaft is part of the Labyrinth, which is very different from the actual underground beneath London. Know what I mean?'

'Not really,' Janey shrugged. 'The thing I want to know is whether you really can travel anywhere in the world from here.'

Cal was about to answer when a voice behind them spoke.

'Of course you can!' it said, high and birdlike, with a strange accent. 'Paris, Sydney, Moscow, you can even get to the South Pole through the Labyrinth. My, my, what a silly question!'

TWENTY-FOUR

Piccadilly

———————

C al and Janey jumped up, ready to run, but their shoes and socks were still by the fire. Without them, their feet would be cut to pieces on shale and rock.

They turned to see a small figure hauling a rowing boat out of the water onto the sand.

'Please don't hurt us,' pleaded Janey. 'We only wanted to get warm. We've been walking for ages and just needed a rest.'

''Urt you?' said the figure, lifting something from the boat before turning to face them. 'Now why on earth would I do something like that?'

Cal found himself looking at an old woman, her thin face a busy road map of lines and wrinkles. She was short, and a long neck and bony hands told them that she was skinny, but she was dressed in so many layers of clothes that she appeared swollen and fat. She wore a dirty old coat that trailed over her feet, which were both wrapped in thick layers of plastic shopping bags and tied off at the tops with string. On her head was a rusty metal helmet that looked like the kind worn by soldiers in the Second World War. The few teeth she had were brown and stubby, and a broken pipe jutted from the corner of her mouth, its cracked bowl smoking lazily. She stared at them, her eyes alert and sharp. Despite her bizarre appearance, she exuded a feeling of harmless energy.

'We heard that the Labyrinth is dangerous,' said Cal.

'Well,' the old woman cheeped, 'there *are* those that would do you 'arm, I suppose. But take it from me, there's as many Upland folk who would do the very same.' She glanced them up and down before continuing. 'I take it that's where you two 'ail from? Upland? Hmmm?'

'Err, yes,' said Cal.

'Been down 'ere long?'

'No, and we don't intend staying too long either,' said Janey. 'It's horrible down here.'

'Now listen 'ere, young missy,' said the old lady, pulling the pipe from her mouth and jabbing its stem towards Janey. 'I don't mind you lot from above comin' down 'ere and traipsing about. It's nice for the company, time to time. But I put me foot down at people saying bad things about the Labyrinth. It's 'ome to some folk, you know.'

'Sorry,' mumbled Janey.

The old woman watched her for a moment and then nodded. She stuck the pipe back in her mouth before making a strange harrumphing noise and waddling towards the fire. At her side, she dragged a basket made of ropes, with what looked like an old hub cap at either end. She set it down and went back to the boat, pulling out a car tyre. Cal and Janey watched, open-mouthed, as she threw it onto the fire, sending a huge plume of thick smoke billowing upwards as the flames licked around the thick rubber.

'Hey, they give off dangerous fumes,' said Cal. 'You shouldn't burn them.'

The old lady thudded cross-legged to the floor and looked up at him.

'Oh yeah? Who says so?' she trilled.

'We learnt it at school. Tyres are a real problem all over the world. Some people are learning to build houses with them, but you shouldn't burn them. It's bad for the environment and makes people sick.'

The old woman shook her head. 'Well, I've been burning them for years and look at me, fit as a fiddle!'

With that, she began inspecting the contents of her basket.

'I think we should get going,' whispered Janey, leaning towards Cal.

'Okay, but give me a minute, I've got an idea.'

He lowered himself to the sand, watching as the strange old woman delved around. Whistling with pleasure, she pulled out a live eel, slick and grey. It thrashed in her hands as she inspected it closely.

'Not bad!' she said, smiling and smashing its head on one of the stones ringing the fire. Cal winced.

'Gross,' muttered Janey.

Next out of the basket came a car number plate, followed by a punctured football. She threw them onto the sand, apparently disinterested in both.

'That's me lot today,' she rasped. 'Now, who's for water worm?'

'What?' said Cal.

She looked at him as though he was mad.

'Water worm!' she cackled, picking up the dead eel and swinging it excitedly round her head like a cowboy twirling a lasso.

'No, thanks,' said Cal, eyeing the eel nervously.

The piercing old eyes flicked to Janey, who was sitting a little further behind Cal. She shook her head without saying anything.

'Suits yerselves then, but don't mind me.'

The woman pulled a rusty knife from her pocket and began hacking at the eel, cutting it into small chunks. She impaled them onto a stick, placing it between the two prongs either side of the fire. The meat began to sizzle above the flames, consumed by thick smoke from the burning tyre.

'The name's Piccadilly,' she said, leaning round the fire and offering a bony hand. Cal shook it.

'Piccadilly?' he asked. 'Like the circus?'

She looked at him strangely.

'What's that? Circus? Are you mad?'

Her voice was piercing, like an incredulous parrot.

'Never mind,' he said quickly. 'My name's Cal and this is Janey.'

Piccadilly offered her hand to Janey, who didn't move but waved at her instead.

'Suits yerself,' said the old woman, winking at her. 'Course, Piccadilly's not me real name, you know. It's just what they call me down 'ere.'

'What is your real name?' asked Cal.

She stared back at him and an odd look crossed her face briefly. It spoke of a longing for strange and distant memories. She fell silent and shook her head.

'Doesn't matter, Piccadilly's me name now, but that's enough about me. Where would you two younglings be 'eaded through the Labyrinth?' she asked, puffing on her pipe.

'We're trying to get to Baker Street.'

'Oh, Baker Street, is it? Up London way?'

'Yes, up London way,' said Cal.

'Important business, is it then?'

'Yeah, it's pretty important. We're trying to find someone.'

'But that don't explain why you're using the Labyrinth to get there, boy,' she said, pointing the pipe at him. 'What's wrong with your Upland pavements?'

'It's complicated. There are people up there who don't like us. They want to hurt us.'

Piccadilly rolled onto her back and burst into a peal of laughter, sending echoes around the cavern. Janey leaned across to Cal.

'She's completely nuts. We're wasting time.'

'I just want to see if she can help us find a way out of here, maybe confirm we're on the right path,' Cal answered.

Janey was about to argue but stopped. Piccadilly was quiet again, watching them suspiciously as she rolled the pipe between her teeth.

'It's rude to whisper when others is present,' she said quietly.

'Sorry,' said Janey, 'but it's rude to laugh at people too.'

'True, missy, very true. But it's 'cos of what you said just now, that you were scared of people trying to 'urts you down 'ere and now you're saying that there are people trying to 'urts you in the Upland too. It seems to me there are people trying to 'urts you two everywhere. So you see, down 'ere ain't too bad after all.'

Piccadilly cackled.

'I was an Uplander once,' the old woman continued. 'Although it was many years ago. That's why old Piccadilly came down 'ere in the first place, as them above were trying to 'urts me. I was on the run and 'ad nowhere else to go you see, and down 'ere I've stayed. Lots of Uplanders come down 'ere to 'ide from those that want to 'urts them, some good, some bad. 'Appier down 'ere though.'

'Your accent's weird. Where did you come from?' asked Janey.

The old woman's eyes clouded, and she frowned.

'A very cold place, a snowy place, a long way from London. I used to live in a big city too, a big, cold city, long time ago now though. Pretty girl I was, in pretty dresses. Very pretty.'

Her voice drifted off and there was that look of longing again, as though she was clinging to something so far away, she could barely recall it.

'We didn't mean to be rude,' said Cal, breaking the silence. 'It's just we were wondering if you could help us.'

''Elp?' the old woman croaked.

'We just want to know if we're on the right path for Baker Street.'

A wisp of smoke curled up from the broken pipe.

'Well, I can 'elp you, of that there's no doubt. But, information begets information, and before I tell you anything, you'll tell me why you need to know. The truth, mind,' she warned.

Cal considered the situation. He was sure he could trust the Pod but time was running out. The old woman seemed harmless enough; true, she was a bit crazy but if she was going to hurt them she could have done it by now.

'I'm going to tell her,' he said to Janey.

'Cal, you can't. Your dad would go mad.'

'Yeah, but like you said earlier, Dad's not here, is he?'

Across the fire, Piccadilly watched them, her eyes two burning coals. She grinned mischievously and tore a piece of half-cooked eel from the spit, gnawing on it hungrily. Cal took a deep breath before speaking.

'My dad is the Aldhelm and he's been kidnapped by a Nephilim. They've captured the Baudouin of France too and we have to give up the Pods. They'll kill both of them if we don't. We've only got until midnight to save them and there are Severals everywhere in London. We're going to see some people at Baker Street who can help us, and we need to know the quickest route. There, that's the truth.'

The old woman's jaw hung open, the half-eaten chunk of eel forgotten in her hand. For a moment there was silence. But then she leaned forward and spoke.

'You're son of the Aldhelm?'

'Yes.'

'Prove it,' she said, throwing the lump of eel into her mouth, sucking and chewing on it noisily.

'What?'

'Prove you're the next in line,' she said, her mouth full. 'If it's for a cause such as you say, then prove to me you're who you say you are.'

'You know about the Pods?'

'Of course I do. Don't everybody?'

Cal reached to unzip his jacket but hesitated. Could he really trust the old woman? Showing her the Pod would reveal its location. What if she was in league with the Nephilim? The Pod wasn't cold, as it was when agents of the Mist were close, but it wasn't warm either. He looked at her rags and soldier's helmet. Surely not.

He pulled out the Pod, and light washed over the island. Piccadilly's eyes grew at the sight of it, reflecting its light across the flames. Her face was like that of a child on Christmas morning, her mouth parted in a beaming smile, revealing the few stumpy teeth that remained. She clasped her hands to her chest, and it seemed as though years of desperate existence fell away from her, leaving her younger. Cal watched the enchantment in her expression and knew that he was looking at someone who valued the Pod and all it stood for. He let her bask in its light for a few moments and then tucked it back inside his coat.

The broad smile stayed on Piccadilly's face and a tear leaked from her eye and ran over her cheek. When she spoke, her voice was calmer than before.

'My, my,' she said. 'That was proof enough. Never did I think I'd see it, not living down 'ere all alone. Thank you, boy, thank you.'

'No problem,' said Cal, encouraged by her reaction. 'Now can you help us and tell us the quickest way to Baker Street?'

'Of course,' she said, pulling herself up and waddling to the water's edge.

''Eads across the cavern directly that way and you'll reach three tunnels. Take the middle one and follow it until you reach a smaller cave, then make sure you take the path straight ahead. After that, take the first left. Can't be more than thirty minutes walking, I reckon.'

'That's it? That'll get us there?'

'If it don't, my name's not Piccadilly,' she said, winking at him.

'Well, that's great, we're pretty close,' Cal said, turning to Janey, who looked less sure. 'Come on, let's get going.'

They were putting on their shoes and socks when Piccadilly made a strange squawking sound and Cal turned round to find her cradling the flask.

'What's in it, boy?' she asked.

'Hot chocolate.'

''Ot chocolate!' she squealed. 'Oh, can I? May I? You've no idea how long it's been since I've tasted it.'

He looked at Janey, who shrugged.

'Go ahead, you can keep it.'

'You are so kind, younglings. ''Ot chocolate! ''Ot chocolate!'

She sang the words in a tuneless warble and began dancing a strange little jig.

'I told you she was completely nuts,' said Janey.

Piccadilly turned sharply.

'But what am I thinking, my fine Upland younglings? I must take you across the water in my boat. Of course I must, after your kindnesses to me.'

'No, honestly, don't worry,' said Cal. 'We can wade through it.'

But the old woman was already shoving the rowing boat into the water, the flask now jutting out of her coat pocket.

'Get in! Get in!' she urged.

The children climbed into the boat, followed by Piccadilly, and sat next to each other on a small bench. It was a tight fit but at least their shoes and socks wouldn't get wet again. The old woman started rowing with surprising strength and the island disappeared quickly, its fire becoming a distant glow once again.

As she rowed, Piccadilly continued her tuneless song about hot chocolate, mostly in English but occasionally veering into another language. She seemed to know exactly where she was going despite the darkness, and after some time stopped rowing, letting the boat drift forward until it nudged against the cave wall.

'There you go, younglings,' Piccadilly said brightly.

Cal drew out the Pod and heard the old woman sigh behind him as its light revealed an opening in the cavern wall.

'Is this the middle tunnel?'

'It is, it certainly is!'

'Well, thanks very much for the advice, and the lift as well.'

'Pleasure, younglings, pleasure.'

Cal and Janey stepped out of the boat, straight up into the dry cave. When they looked back, the old woman was cradling the flask as though it was a baby, speaking quietly.

'Such a cold city, 'ot chocolate was wonderful, a treat. Such pretty dresses and beautiful people and fine palaces, but so cold, so cold.'

'Piccadilly?' said Janey.

The old woman looked up.

'What was your real name? You know, when you were in the cold place?'

'Well, let me see, missy. I've not used it for such a long time, and I did wear such pretty dresses, you know, just like a fairy story. That was before the devils came, before they tried to 'urts me. Down 'ere is safer, down 'ere is right.'

Her voice drifted off and she looked at the flask. When the children tried to say goodbye, she didn't acknowledge them.

'Come on,' said Cal. 'We should go.'

They hadn't taken ten paces when the old woman's voice chimed up behind them brightly.

'Anastasia!' she cried. 'My name was Anastasia.'

Cal looked back at the cave mouth but the boat had gone. In the distance, oars were dipping in and out of water. He listened until he could hear them no more and then he and Janey turned away, leaving the water-filled cavern behind them.

*

Sometime later, back on the sandy island, the old woman cradled the flask as tears ran down her face.

'Bless the younglings and their kindness. Piccadilly sent them on their path. Piccadilly did what the Pod boy asked. She did what 'e wanted, but if only 'e 'ad asked for the safest path, not the quickest.'

She rocked back and forth and stroked the flask.

'Such pretty dresses, but so cold,' she muttered in the darkness.

TWENTY-FIVE

Ambush

C al was sure it was getting harder to see but he didn't want to worry Janey, so said nothing. If Piccadilly was right, they had less than a thirty-minute walk ahead of them and he wanted to focus on getting out of the Labyrinth as quickly as possible.

The tunnel eventually emerged into another cave, smaller this time. Three openings gaped in its walls, one straight ahead and one each to the left and right, just as Piccadilly had described. Go straight ahead, she had said. But before they could take a step, a noise from the left-hand passage caused them to stop. A strange snapping, repeating every few seconds, accompanied by a bellowing voice, deep and primal. The children hovered in the tunnel mouth before ducking back inside it. Cal shoved the Pod inside his coat and they crouched down in the darkness.

A faint light appeared in the opening, growing steadily brighter, seeping out into the cave. Neither of them breathed as four figures emerged. Man-shaped but about half Cal's height, they were scrawny, with balding heads and pale, hairless skin that was covered in welts and scars. Their facial features were small and sharp; the eyes and mouths centred around long, hooked noses. Their ears were gunk-encrusted holes. They wore nothing but ragged loincloths and walked side by side in pairs, each couple working as a team, straining at ropes that passed over their shoulders.

The ropes were connected to a wooden platform that emerged in the cavern, gliding slowly across a series of wooden rollers. A lantern hung from each corner. Two more of the strange figures appeared from the tunnel, scampering along behind, picking up the used rollers and placing them ahead of the platform so that it could continue its progress. In the low light, Cal could see something lying on its surface. It resembled an enormous slug, a glistening lump of gristle, bereft of any discernible features. Its sides heaved as the pale-skinned creatures strained on the ropes. Behind it came more of them, using long poles to push the back of the platform, leaning against them with their wiry bodies, grimacing with effort.

What came next was a being that caused Cal and Janey to grab hold of each other tightly in the darkness.

It had been constricted in the tunnel, but once in the cavern, unfurled to almost ten feet in height. It stood on two legs, with the body of a human and the head of a bull. Horns, thicker than Cal's arms, spiralled up from its head, and a taut, barrel-like chest rippled with muscle. Covered in bushy brown hair, its hooves sparked as they cracked against the rock floor. Leathery wings sprouted from its shoulders and began to beat slowly in the freedom of the cave.

The beast flicked its wrist and a whip cracked across the back of one of the skinny creatures that was pushing with all its might against a pole. It let out a thin wail and collapsed to its knees. Bull-head towered over it and snorted. A huge glob of snot dropped from its snout onto the cavern floor. It then launched a powerful kick at the kneeling figure, sending it flying through the cave and crashing against the wall, before striding after the strange procession into the opposite passage, bending low and out of sight. The crack of the whip and bellowing continued, steadily growing faint. Cal and Janey sat huddled together, saying nothing until everything was completely quiet.

'What the hell was that?' whispered Janey eventually.

'No idea,' answered Cal. 'I'm just glad it didn't spot us.'

He crawled forward, listening carefully. Bull-head and the grotesque parade had gone. He pulled out the Pod and light outlined the small body at the base of the wall.

'I'm going to check it out. You coming?' he said, turning back to Janey.

She nodded and together they crossed to where the creature lay. It was face down, arms spread, its legs buckled beneath it. Fine wisps of hair jutted from the back of its head. The lash marks from the whip were vivid and glistened under the Podlight.

'It could do with a wash,' said Janey, wrinkling her nose.

'Poor thing,' said Cal. 'However bad it smells or looks, nothing deserves to be treated like that.'

'True, but don't you think we'd better get going, in case that bull thing comes back?'

'Yeah, I just want to check its pulse, assuming it's got one.'

Cal took the twig-like wrist in his fingers. The skin reminded him of the time he'd touched an elephant at the zoo; dry and tough. At first, he couldn't feel anything but then, very slightly, he felt a faint drumming. He moved his fingers and there it was again, stronger now and beating impossibly fast.

'It's alive,' he whispered.

Janey was about to reply when the creature jumped up, pointed yellow teeth bared, hissing and spitting. It leapt at Cal, throwing him onto his back, clawing at him viciously. Cal pushed with all his might to hold it off and the two of them rolled violently on the floor. Janey tried to grab one of its arms but it shook her off, hurling her to the ground. She looked around desperately for a weapon and noticed a pile of rocks on the opposite side of the cave. Jumping up, she made a dash for it, scrabbling through the rubble, trying to find something large enough.

'Ja… n… ey… Hee… eeellp!' Cal called.

Bony fingers were around his neck, squeezing hard. Janey grabbed the nearest stone and ran back to the fight.

'Let him go!' she cried.

The creature ignored her and she raised the stone above her head.

'I said let him go!'

The thing trained its beady eyes on her, hissing loudly, before turning back to Cal.

Janey brought the stone down on the back of its head as hard as she could. Cal heard a dull cracking sound. For a moment, it didn't react, but then it unleashed a howl of pain and let him go. It leapt up and ran across the cavern shrieking, holding its hands to its bleeding head. Stopping to flash a last furious gaze back at them, it screamed bitterly before diving into the tunnel along which Bull-head and the procession had disappeared. Janey stared after it, breathing hard.

'Thanks,' said Cal, his voice hoarse.

Janey dropped the stone and knelt next to him. 'Are you okay?'

'A bit sore but that's all.'

'Can you move?'

Cal nodded and Janey helped him onto his feet.

'Right, no more heroics. Let's just get out of here.'

'Deal,' he said.

His skin burned where the creature had gripped him, and his throat felt like he'd swallowed barbed wire. Whatever it was, he was glad to see the back of it. Janey was right; the sooner they were out of here, the better.

'Can you run?' he asked.

'If it means we get out of here quicker then yeah, I can run.'

They started to jog, taking care on the uneven floor, making for the middle passage. The further they went, the weaker the Podlight seemed to get.

'Is it me or is it getting darker?' panted Janey.

Cal didn't reply; he was too busy looking for the turning on the left as per Piccadilly's directions. But the passage stretched ahead of them with no openings on either side. He was about to suggest they slowed for safety, when his shin collided with something and he was sent sprawling, smacking his head painfully as he landed. A shriek from Janey, followed by a thud, told him she'd done the same. Cal lay stunned as figures moved out of the shadows, surrounding them. Rough hands hauled him onto his feet.

'Hey!' exclaimed Janey. 'Get off me. GET OFF!'

Her voice became muffled and then fell silent. Cal, too dazed to struggle, felt his legs give way before he knew no more.

TWENTY-SIX
Making A Deal

———

A throbbing pain attacked Cal's skull from every angle. Somewhere distant was the sound of muffled voices. He strained to hear them clearly.

Opening his eyes, they took time to adjust, focusing on jagged rock. It flickered and shifted, bathed in firelight. Men and women, their voices clearer now, fought to be heard. Cal flexed his hands and feet; he could feel no bindings.

'There you go, miss,' growled a voice. 'Eat up and you'll soon feel better.'

'Mmmm, thanks. That's really tasty.'

Cal recognised Janey's voice and sat up, the ache in his head spinning into dizziness that blurred his vision.

'Janey?' he called out.

There was a pause.

'Cal!' cried Janey. He felt arms around his neck,

hugging him close. 'You're awake. I was worried. Twilight's here too. They found her.'

Cal pushed Janey away as something jumped into his lap. He looked down to see the black and white Chattan looking up at him through wide eyes.

'Twilight, thank God,' he said, gathering her in his arms and letting tears of relief flow into her fur. She purred as he held her, not wanting to let go.

'They said they know you,' whispered Janey.

Cal looked up and saw they were in a small cave. A fire burned at its centre. Above the flames, a large black pot steamed and bubbled like a witch's cauldron. Sitting around it were no fewer than ten people, dressed in dark clothes. Where it showed, their skin was covered in tattoos. Most of them had shaved heads and various piercings through their ears, noses and lips. They stared at him, unsmiling.

'Well, 'ello there, young Cal,' boomed a deep voice. 'What a surprise to find you daan 'ere.'

A silhouette leaned forward and Cal saw a single eye shine and a bald head glint in the light of the fire. It was Baron. Cal swallowed.

'We've been followin' yer for a bit. Didn't know it was you o' course. We found yer Chattan a few passageways back. Yer should take more care of 'er. She's valuable, yer know.'

'Twilight, I'm so sorry,' said Cal, stroking her.

'Ah, now ain't that sweet,' said Baron, provoking a round of laughter from the other pirates. Twilight growled and glared at them. Cal held her to him and felt furious tension pulse through her body.

'Thanks for taking care of her,' he said.

'No problem. Let's just say you owe me,' replied Baron, winking. 'Ow's yer 'ead?'

'It's okay, hurting a bit.'

'I'm not surprised. That was a fair smack.'

'It wouldn't have happened if you hadn't tripped us.'

'Yeah, sorry about that. Can't say I'm 'appy about it meself. I fought we'd snagged someone wiv some loot. The Labyrinth 'as been very profitable for us in the past.'

Baron grinned as bowls were filled with ladles of thick, steaming liquid and passed around.

'You should have some food,' suggested Janey. 'You're a bit pale.'

'Not for me,' said Cal.

'Some water then,' offered Baron, holding out a dented tin mug.

Cal hesitated.

'It's water, that's all,' Baron insisted. 'Blimey, someone's jumpy.'

Cal took a cautious sip before draining the rest in one swig. The icy liquid shocked his body into life as it went down. Baron smiled.

'How long have we been here?' asked Cal.

'It's an hour since you smacked yer bonce,' barked another pirate. Cal thought it might have been a woman but wasn't sure.

'That's long enough,' he said, standing up from the bed of furs, fighting the wave of nausea that threatened to engulf him. 'We've got to go.'

'Cal, don't you think they could help us?' said Janey.

'No way,' he said, glancing at the pirates as they slurped stew noisily. Baron was picking at his teeth with a rusty knife, pretending to ignore them.

'But with that horrible bull thing out there, maybe we'd be safer sticking with these guys. I know they're a bit… well, rough, but still.'

'We can't trust them.'

'What did you say?' said Baron, glancing up at Janey. 'Pardon?'

'What did you just say?' he said again, pushing himself up under the weight of his hunchback. 'Sommat about a bull?'

'Well, yeah, we saw something, I don't know what. It had wings and a bull's head. It wasn't far from where you tripped us up.'

'Bloody 'ell!' said Baron, shaking his head. 'You *are* lucky, ain't yer?'

'What do you mean?' asked Cal.

'You saw the Minotaur, thass what I mean.'

'Minotaur?'

'Yeah, and you're damn lucky to 'ave survived. What was it doin'?'

As Janey described the scene Baron listened, grinding his teeth at the description of the giant slug. Behind him, the river pirates exchanged nervous glances.

'They was gonna feed on that thing. They breed 'em for food. My, my, it's rare for the Minotaur to be seen these days. Sommat's goin' on.'

'Could it be linked to the Mist?' asked Janey.

Cal elbowed her in the ribs and she clamped a hand to her mouth.

'What's that?' said Baron.

'Nothing, forget it,' Cal said hurriedly.

'Now listen 'ere, we've taken good care of you two since we found yer and I fink you owe us an explanation as to why yer daan 'ere.' He drew something from his pocket. 'And perhaps you'd like to tell me why the Aldhelm left you alone with this?'

He let the Pod dangle from his fingers, grey and lifeless. Twilight yowled and hissed. Cal snatched a hand to his neck but felt nothing. Baron must have taken it when he was unconscious.

'Give that back!' he shouted.

'I don't fink so, son,' said Baron. 'Not until you tell me what's goin' on.'

Cal lunged for the Pod, grasping at it with his fingers, but Baron sidestepped lithely and he missed. Within moments, the pirates were on their feet and Cal was hauled up in a strong grip, his arms pinned to his sides and a knife at his throat. Janey ran forward but was pulled back by the shaven-headed woman who had spoken earlier. Several large pieces of metal skewered her nose. Twilight thrashed and twisted, caught in the hands of another pirate, her limbs trapped against his chest and her claws rendered useless.

'Right,' said Baron, 'I fink you'd better start talkin' or you might not see *these* again.'

He reached into another pocket and brought out the second Pod.

'What? How?' gasped Janey.

'Sorry, miss, it's kind of a bad 'abit,' said Baron, smiling mischievously.

Janey stared at Cal miserably and he looked across to Baron and nodded, his shoulders slumping.

'That's better,' said Baron. He waved a hand and the children were released. 'Now mind you leave nuffin' out, Wainwright, or I'll know.'

Baron took a seat and Cal began the tale with Twilight nestled against him. He started with Baron's visit to *Podwitch* just days before, continuing through everything that had happened in between, right up until they had seen the Minotaur. Baron licked his lips.

'Well, well, well. You two really are in trouble, Jeb too by all accounts,' he said. 'I'd never 'ave believed any of it without finding the Pods on yer. I know the Aldhelm never lets it out of 'is sight. Much too risky. Wouldn't 'ave done that for no good reason. And now you say you're on your way to Baker Street?'

'Yes,' said Cal, 'but I think we're too late. There can't be much time until daylight.'

'Can you help us?' asked Janey.

The river pirate turned to her. 'Now 'old on a minute, why would I want to get involved? It's not my problem, see?'

'Of course it's your problem!' gasped Janey. 'Haven't you listened to anything Cal's said? The whole world could be in danger from this Mist stuff. The Nephi-thingies are really powerful and this bull-headed Mino-whatsit is walking around down here for the first time in ages with its vicious little slaves. And you say it's not your problem?'

'Listen to me,' growled Baron. 'It's only my problem if I let it be. The way I see it, it's more of an opportunity.'

'An opportunity?' asked Cal. 'How?'

'Well, look at the situation,' said Baron, stroking his chin. 'This Nephilim, Thorne, is lookin' pretty powerful in my book. And your dad's in a bad way, wiv only you kids and a Chattan to 'elp 'im. At the end of the day, it's me who's got the Pods now, ain't it? So I reckon that puts me in a pretty good position. I'm sure that the Nephilim would be interested in a deal that would see me very well off for a long, long time.'

'You wouldn't,' cried Janey. 'You couldn't.'

The pirate looked at Cal in amusement and Cal saw he was serious. Baron was more than capable of using this as a situation he and his crew could exploit. The others sniggered at Janey's outburst.

'May I speak with you alone, Baron?' said a voice.

It was small, but firm enough to silence the laughter. Baron's smile froze and he glanced down to where Twilight was sitting, watching him.

'What's this?' Baron said. 'It's outside yer hours, Chattan. ''Asn't the cat still got yer tongue?'

Another burst of laughter broke out and Twilight stared at him coldly.

'The curse has no power over my kind in the Labyrinth,' she replied. 'Sometimes I simply choose not to talk unless absolutely necessary.'

Cal's jaw hung open.

'Now that's a first,' said Baron.

'You owe it to the boy's parents to listen,' said Twilight. '*Both* of them.'

Something in her tone caught the pirate's attention and his gaze shifted down to his fingers.

'Come on then,' he said. 'What is it you want?'

'Alone,' said the cat.

Baron knew that when Chattan spoke, they did not waste words.

He gestured across the cave.

'Over 'ere,' he said.

They moved away and the pirate crouched down, allowing the cat to speak quietly into his ear. Cal watched the conversation closely.

Baron nodded, occasionally shaking his head and only speaking briefly when Twilight was done. After less than ten minutes, the conversation was over and Twilight made her way back to Cal. Baron remained where he was, deep in thought. A hush had descended over the cave and the pirates watched him impatiently, flashing angry glances at the Chattan.

Eventually, Baron stood up as tall as his hunchback would allow.

'Our plan 'as changed,' he said. 'We're gonna take a different course.'

The pirates murmured in disapproval, but Baron waved away their complaints.

'A new deal will bring us just as many riches as our previous plan, per'aps more. On that, I 'ave the Chattan's promise,' he said, pointing at Twilight. 'And we all know that a Chattan's word is as strong as oak.' He lifted the Pods and held them out. Cal and Janey stared at him uncertainly. 'Well, come on you two. What are you waitin' for? You wanna get goin', right?'

Cal crossed the cave and took the Pods. Jeb's sparked into life at his touch, its light causing the pirates to shrink back against the wall; all but Baron, who stared at it greedily. For a moment, his grip tightened on them, refusing to let go. But then his eye closed and he let the necklaces slip from his hand.

Cal passed Legard's Pod to Janey and she put it round her neck, tucking it into her coat. Cal did the same, concealing the Podlight once more. The cave was silent.

'All right, you lot, let's be makin' a move,' Baron yelled. 'These kids 'ave an appointment to keep at Baker Street.'

The river pirates leapt up, kicking sand over the fire and shoving belongings into sacks. Cal held open his backpack for Twilight, who clambered in.

'Thanks, Baron,' said Cal, approaching the pirate.

'Don't thank me, boy. Thank the cat,' said Baron, tying on a grubby cloak.

Cal heard Twilight purring gently behind him and moved away.

'Dad said never to trust the pirates, Twilight,' he whispered.

'And he's right. But Baron won't give us any problems now. Besides, we have no choice. If the Minotaur is on the move, others will be too.'

'What did you say to him?'

'It doesn't matter. Let's just say that we have made a deal. Don't worry, I'll keep an eye on him.'

'Okay, I hope you're right.'

Within seconds, the cave was dark, apart from a couple of lanterns held high by the pirates.

'Follow me,' said Baron. He looked at Cal and Janey. 'You two stay close.'

He ducked through a low opening in the cave wall. Cal and Janey were next, followed by the others.

They emerged in a passageway and moved in single file, passing two cross-tunnels, turning left at the third. Baron scuttled ahead quickly, often disappearing from sight but always reappearing from the darkness.

'One left turn up ahead and we're almost there,' he growled.

'Great!' said Janey. 'I just want to see daylight again.'

Baron flashed a grimace at her and was about to turn away when a screech echoed behind them, sounding like the cry of a giant bird of prey. Another, then another, then another followed it, each wail adding to the previous one, building into a deafening crescendo. The pirates whirled around, swords and knives hissing from their scabbards. Baron stared along the tunnel.

'It sounds like the thing that attacked you in the cave,' cried Janey.

'What thing?' barked Baron.

'One of those horrible creatures the Minotaur left half dead. It tried to kill Cal until I injured it and it ran away.'

'What? Yer let it go?' said Baron.

The piercing shrieks were approaching rapidly, bouncing off the walls, seeming to come at them from every direction.

'Yeah, why?' shouted Janey above the noise.

Baron drew his sword. 'We 'ave to get out of 'ere. They're lookin' for yer. Lots of 'em.'

'Who're looking for us?' said Cal, grabbing Baron's arm.

'Redcaps. Flesh eaters,' hissed the pirate. 'I'm surprised it took 'em this long. Come on!'

He strode ahead and the children followed, running to keep up. The ear-splitting screeches were now accompanied by the sound of bare feet slapping on rock. Cal glanced back and saw countless silhouettes scurrying along the tunnel behind them. Pirate lanterns picked out flashes of pale skin in the gloom.

'SPEARS!' cried one of the pirates.

Something flew by Cal's head, clattering off the rock wall to his right. The sound of running feet came to a halt and Baron swung round. The pirates at the rear had turned to face their pursuers, pointing their swords at the figures in the darkness. The Redcaps hovered, chittering like bats. Exuding malevolent rage, their eyes glinted like dark flints in the lamplight and their obnoxious stink filled the tunnel.

'Steady!' cried Baron. 'No sudden moves!'

A spear flew out of the tunnel, slamming one of the pirates to the floor with a cry that died in his throat. The others needed no more provocation and leapt forward with angry yells. The Redcaps surged to meet them and the sound of metal clashing on bone echoed sickeningly about them.

'In 'ere!' shouted Baron, pushing Cal and Janey through an opening in the rock at the side of the tunnel. 'Move as fast as you can to the end and climb quickly. You'll come out near Baker Street. Just pray the Minotaur doesn't show. We'll soon catch you up.'

He ducked back into the corridor and his voice bellowed over the shrieks of the Redcaps.

'Come on!' cried Cal, grabbing Janey and pulling her along the passage.

The sounds of battle faded as they ran. Cal wondered just how far they had to go. He stumbled down on one knee but used his momentum to push himself up and forward again. His eyes eventually fixed on something in the distance and as they got nearer, he saw a ladder, just like the one they had descended from *Podwitch*, running up the wall in front of them. As they arrived at it, a blood-curdling scream came up the tunnel behind them.

'You first. Hurry!' he cried, breathless.

Janey didn't argue and climbed quickly. Cal followed, his tired and aching limbs forgotten.

The climb may or may not have been as long as the initial descent from *Podwitch*, although it seemed much quicker when Janey called down to him.

'I'm here. This is the top, I think.'

Cal came up close behind her and held up the Podlight, revealing a square slab of concrete above the ladder.

'It won't budge,' Janey said, pushing up against it. 'But

I'm so tired, I don't even know if I've got the strength to lift it.'

'Keep trying,' Cal urged.

But it was no good; it wouldn't move.

'Wait a minute, I need to unlock the Podhex.' Cal gripped the Pod and closed his eyes, uttering his mum's name. 'Now try,' he called up.

Janey pushed, but the gateway remained shut.

'Come on!' she cried.

A sudden jerking movement from below shocked Cal and he gripped the rungs tightly.

'What's that?' squealed Janey.

'It's nothing, just concentrate,' said Cal.

He kept his voice calm, although the thought of a Redcap climbing up from below was more than he could stand.

'I've got an idea!' said Janey. 'Maybe you need to touch the gateway for the Podmagic to work. Like you held the corner of the rug.'

'But I can't reach past you.'

The ladder shook more forcefully beneath them.

'Grab hold of my leg and I'll touch the door,' yelled Janey. 'Maybe that'll be enough. Let's try it.'

Cal held the rung and Pod with one hand, grasping Janey's leg with the other. The ladder jolted as something climbed closer.

'Ready?' he called up.

'Yep.'

Cal closed his eyes and focused on the Pod, blocking out all thoughts of Minotaurs, Redcaps and Piccadilly on her island. He waited until calm had descended before speaking his mum's name under his breath. Cal felt a blast of air as the slab above them opened a chink.

'That's it,' cried Janey a second later.

She pushed further and the concrete lifted easily, letting dingy London light flood into the shaft. She moved up and out before calling back down.

'Come on, Cal, you're not gonna believe this.'

Another jerk on the ladder shocked Cal into moving and he hauled himself up the last ten rungs.

He emerged through the floor of an old-fashioned red phone box. Its concrete base was propped up against the glass. Janey was standing outside, holding the door open. Cal stepped up and out onto the pavement. Without thinking, he ducked back inside to slam down the concrete slab, but then hesitated and glanced at Janey.

'What about Baron and the others?'

'I dunno, but we can't leave it open.'

Cal knelt and leaned over the shaft. Deep down, he could just make out a bald head climbing up from the darkness.

'Baron,' he called. 'Is that you?'

The figure stopped climbing and glanced up, revealing a flash of malevolent eyes. The Redcap hissed and began climbing again, moving swiftly.

Cal grabbed the concrete slab in both hands, and with a final glance down to the fiendish face, slammed it shut. He rested his palm against it and whispered his mum's name before letting the phone box door swing shut on the Labyrinth and its hideous inhabitants below.

TWENTY-SEVEN

221b Baker Street

They left the phone box and walked quickly, while trying to remain as inconspicuous as possible. The pre-dawn light was murky, and frost lay over London's pavements like icing sugar on a Christmas cake. Things were strangely quiet; there were no people or traffic. Sirens howled in the distance and somewhere nearby a helicopter hovered low in the sky.

'What's going on?' said Janey. 'It should be busier than this.'

'Something's wrong,' said Cal.

Turning north on Baker Street, they passed several doorways, scanning the building numbers.

'This is it,' he said, pointing to a tall terraced redbrick house.

At ground level was a shop window and a sign, which read: *The Sherlock Holmes Museum*, in gold letters on a green background. A blue plaque, set into the wall between the two rectangular windows on the first floor, had *221b* written on it in large white letters.

'Can you help me with the rucksack?'

Janey eased it off his back and set it down on the pavement. Twilight skipped out and stretched.

'I bet you're happy to be out of there,' said Cal, scratching her neck. 'But I still don't get what you said to Baron to make him help us.'

The Chattan wound through his legs, purring loudly. She even nuzzled up against Janey's ankle and let her run a hand down her back before darting away in the direction of Regent's Park.

'Twilight?' Cal called, alarmed to see her leaving.

She stopped and turned briefly. Then she was gone, slinking under a parked car and out of sight. Cal moved to follow her but stopped as Janey reached a hand to his arm.

'Come on, Cal, we've got to hurry. It's nearly six o'clock. Wherever Twilight's going, she'll be fine. She probably needs to be on her own after being in the Labyrinth.'

'Yeah,' said Cal. 'I guess you're right.'

He stared after the Chattan before turning towards 221b Baker Street, grasping Janey's hand in his. He raised the Pod up and waited.

A movement caused Janey to turn. A car was entering the northern end of the street. It slowed as it approached them and she saw something on its roof.

'Cal,' she hissed. 'It's the police. I think they're watching us!'

'Keep looking at the museum.'

The police car passed behind them. The blue glow had appeared at the heart of the Pod, accompanied by the strange rushing sound that Cal remembered from Doughty Street. Janey glanced to the left and saw that the police car was now turning in the road.

'They're coming back.'

The sound of rushing water grew louder and the Podlight was vibrant. It spread down to the paving slabs, across to the front of the building and then ran vertically up the front wall. As it reached the plaque, a beam of light shot from the Pod towards it, and the sound became a deafening roar. A policeman was out of the car now and frowning at them as Janey put her hand to her ear and Cal winced at the noise.

Suddenly Baker Street was no longer there, and they were suspended in front of 221b, their senses alive with the noise and light all about them. Janey squeezed Cal's hand and he squeezed back reassuringly. And then it was gone and they were on the pavement once more, silence ringing in their ears.

'We're not doing anything wrong. It's for a school project,' came Janey's voice.

She was facing the policeman, who was staring at them, a strange look on his face. He blinked and shook his head.

'What's up with him?' said Janey, puzzled.

'He can't see us,' said Cal. 'We're not *there* anymore because we're *here* now, outside time. He's going to be very confused.'

'You mean we just disappeared?'

Cal nodded.

They watched the two policemen have a conversation before proceeding to inspect the street, looking behind waste bins and beneath parked cars.

'Cool!' Janey said, beaming. 'For a minute, I thought we were in trouble.'

Cal jogged forward to the door of 221b. He pounded on it and stepped back. Almost immediately the door was whipped open violently. Light from within silhouetted a tall figure in a long dressing gown. Prominent, pointed features frowned down at them from an intelligent face.

Cal flashed a glance at Janey, who was staring up at the figure, her mouth gaping.

'Could you be... I mean... are you... Sherlock Holmes?' Cal asked.

The man, who looked remarkably like pictures of the detective Cal had glimpsed in books, twitched his head in a curt nod as he glared back at Janey. His eyes ran her up and down, as sharp as an eagle.

'Hello,' she whispered.

'You are an only child and used to play the piano, but gave up through boredom, coupled with a desire to spend more time outside,' said Sherlock Holmes, raising an eyebrow. 'You wish to be a mountain climber when you grow up and are secretly hoping to receive a new bicycle for your next birthday.' Janey could do nothing but stare back at him and nod. 'Now come inside quickly, there is much to discuss and little time. Make your way upstairs to the front room. I shall follow you presently.'

They stepped into the hallway. Gas lamps hissed on the walls, giving off a grimy yellow light as Cal led the way up the red-carpeted stairs. The house was neat and tidy but had little decoration. They followed the landing round towards the front of the building, passing two doors on the right. Light under the oak panelled door at which they arrived told them the room was occupied.

'Ready?' Cal asked.

Janey nodded and put a hand on his arm. 'Do you know who's going to be in there?'

'No idea.'

'Cal, this is pretty amazing, isn't it?'

'Yeah, it is, but let's just try and act normal, okay?'

'Okay.'

He raised his hand to knock but the door swung open before he could. There stood Charles Dickens, a cigarette burning in his hand and concern on his face. His countenance softened when he saw Cal.

'My dear Master Wainwright,' he said, holding out a hand. Cal shook it, relief flooding through him at the sight of the deceased novelist.

'Hello, Mr Dickens, it's good to see you.'

'We were concerned for you. As it is, you have barely made it in time.'

'We'd have been quicker, but Dad and Monsieur Legard have been captured by the Nephilim. We had to come through the Labyrinth.'

Charles Dickens' eyes widened in surprise and then hardened. 'My boy, I had no idea. You must come in and get warm, both of you.' His eyes registered Janey for the first time. 'And who, may I ask, is your brave companion?'

Janey stared at him silently.

'Oh yeah, sorry,' said Cal. 'This is—'

'Janey, my name's Janey,' she finished for him. 'I'm a friend of Cal's.'

'Well, Miss Janey, anyone who is a friend of the future Aldhelm, is a friend of the brethren of the Blue Plaques.'

Mr Dickens stood to one side, ushering them into the front room where two tall rectangular windows overlooked the street. Vivid crimson paper covered the walls, which were lined with all manner of pictures and yellowed newspaper cuttings. On one wall, three daggers were mounted above one another on small hooks. A fireplace stood in the middle of the wall to the left, its embers glowing comfortingly. The mantel shelf over it was scattered with papers, pictures, tools and a gun. An old slipper hung beneath. To the end of the room furthest from the windows stood a dark wooden table. It was covered in an array of glass tubes and flasks, some with strange coloured liquid inside, others bubbling gently. The air was smoky, and thick with the odour of scientific experiments, cigarettes, pipes and cigars.

Facing the fire were two people, sitting with their backs to the children.

'My friends,' said Charles Dickens, guiding the children to the warm hearth. 'I would like to introduce you to the son of the Aldhelm, Master Cal Wainwright, and his friend, Miss Janey. They have undertaken a journey through the Labyrinth to join us for this emergency meeting, so please be gentle.'

A man and a woman looked Cal and Janey up and down, their faces a mixture of stern inspection and kindness.

'Children, these are fellow members of the Plaque Network,' said Mr Dickens.

In an armchair sat a gruff-looking older man who was smoking a fat cigar, its thick smoke curling lazily above his head. His dark blue suit had a thick pinstripe running through it. A black bowler hat sat on a small table next to his chair. His eyes were hard but not without humour.

'Mr Winston Churchill,' said Dickens. 'I'm sure he needs no further introduction. A man whose involvement in the last significant uprising of the Mist speaks volumes of his value to our cause.'

Janey and Cal took turns shaking Winston Churchill's chubby hand. His grip was as firm as the look in his eye. He grunted curtly.

'You have the look of your father, which means you'll need toughening up. Not like your grandmother. Now *there* was an Aldhelm. Let's hope you take after her,' he grumbled, eyeing Cal up and down. 'So, are you up for the fight of your life, boy?'

'Yes,' said Cal.

'Good, because it will not be over quickly and will be hard on us all. Lives will be lost and danger will be commonplace. But together, we can achieve. Together, we *must* achieve.'

'Yes,' Cal repeated, not knowing what else to say.

Winston Churchill nodded, turning his gaze to the embers in the fireplace.

Mr Dickens gestured to the second figure facing them. It was a woman. She was very old and wore a long black dress. A white bonnet covered her hair. Long, delicate fingers were clasped in her lap. Her eyes spoke of both strength and sadness, but above all, great compassion.

'This is Miss Florence Nightingale, whose services on the field of battle, conducted with bravery and expert knowledge of medicine, brought her to the network,' said Mr Dickens proudly.

Florence Nightingale offered her hand and the children shook it. 'Such brave children to have journeyed through the Labyrinth,' she said quietly. 'You are a credit to your father, Master Wainwright, you and your young friend here.'

'Thank you,' said Cal.

Standing in front of such legendary figures was humbling and Cal felt huge waves of relief at their presence. Somehow, having made it this far seemed to have made the chances of rescuing his dad and the Baudouin much greater.

Before anyone else could speak, Sherlock Holmes swept through the door in a whirl of dressing gown and cigarette smoke, slamming it shut behind him. He threw himself into an armchair, drawing his knees up to his chin and staring at the children through piercing eyes.

'Honestly, Holmes, I do wish you wouldn't slam doors all the time. It does play on my nerves,' said Charles Dickens.

Sherlock Holmes ignored him and continued his examination of Cal and Janey.

'What has been determined so far?' he asked.

'We have just finished introductions, Sherlock,' said Miss Nightingale.

'What, pray tell, is the delay?' asked the detective. 'Let us proceed and please, ensure accuracy on each and every fact.'

'Hear! Hear!' barked Winston Churchill.

Weary but encouraged, Cal told his story for the second time in recent hours. Janey insisted on relaying her own experiences and even Holmes and Churchill appeared amused by her enthusiasm.

Dickens stood and poured hot tea from a pot as they spoke, handing cups to Cal and Janey, as well as a plate of buttered toast. After they had eaten, Cal described their journey through the Labyrinth and subsequent arrival near Baker Street.

'Ah, yes,' said Florence Nightingale. 'You would do well to remember that each and every red phone box across England marks an entrance and exit from the Labyrinth. Any that were destroyed and replaced with those loathsome new glass and plastic ones were never Labyrinth gateways in the first place.'

'So that's everything,' said Cal, when all was told.

'And we only have until midnight,' added Janey.

The Blue Plaque brethren watched them silently, shrouded in smoke.

'What a remarkable tale,' said Miss Nightingale.

'Indeed,' added Holmes, 'but it leaves us with quite a

problem. In fact, I would go so far as to say that it is most definitely a three-pipe problem.'

He leapt up and darted to the fireplace. Scooping a handful of tobacco from the old slipper, he packed it into a long-stemmed pipe, which he lit with a flourish before returning to his chair. He closed his eyes and puffed furiously.

'We knew something was wrong,' said Florence Nightingale. 'We had repeatedly summoned the Aldhelm but received no response until yesterday, in your time, that is. I think I may be right in saying that this would be a first. Gentlemen?'

Winston Churchill grunted and Charles Dickens nodded. 'You're right, Florence,' he said. 'Things look grave for us if the Mist has found a way to interfere with our communications.'

'Have you seen more Severals outside time?' asked Cal.

'Indeed,' said Mr Dickens. 'It seems all we can do is move from residence to residence in an attempt to avoid their attentions. There would have been far more of us to greet you had it not been for other members working to distract the Severals throughout the network.'

'Our primary concern is the safety of the Pods,' growled Winston Churchill. 'We must remember that their Guardians are essentially expendable. At least we know where the Pods are and that they are safe. Whether or not it would be wise to even attempt a rescue of Wainwright and Legard, should be the topic of conversation.'

'But we have to rescue them!' cried Janey. 'We can't just leave—'

She stopped as Cal laid a hand on her shoulder.

'Mr Churchill,' he said carefully. 'I don't want to upset you, but I disagree. I think that if we leave them with Thorne and the Severals, it would make us look weak. Surely it's worth showing them we're not afraid. If Thorne suspects the next Aldhelm is prepared to give up his dad and the Baudouin without a fight, that doesn't say much for the future, does it?

'I think that now's the time to show we're not going to roll over and do what they want. Saving Dad and Monsieur Legard would be a heck of a way to show them we mean business.'

Winston Churchill watched him through a fog of cigar smoke. He nodded and flashed a brief smile.

Each member of the Blue Plaque Network took turns to ask questions, which the children answered as best they could. Eventually, Cal felt his eyelids closing. He sat up in an attempt to fight the tiredness but lack of sleep and all they had been through soon caught up with him. Both he and Janey began to doze in front of the fire, leaning on each other awkwardly.

Gentle hands lifted them to their feet, guiding them into a back room, where two single beds with crisp sheets were waiting. Cal fell into one without undressing. His last thought was of how hard and lumpy the mattress felt beneath him, but it made no difference and soon he plunged into a deep sleep.

TWENTY-EIGHT

A Course Of Action

Florence Nightingale woke Cal and Janey with hot cups of tea. Tendrils of steam curled upwards from them like beckoning fingers.

'We are ready to propose a course of action to you, Master Wainwright. Please, drink your tea and join us when you're ready,' she said.

'What time is it?' asked Cal.

'In the real London, it is a little after eight o'clock.'

'In the evening?'

'Indeed. You have both slept for the day and I hope are feeling the benefit of your rest.'

'But I thought time didn't move while we were here, and we'd be going back at the same time we left?'

'Well, that is true,' Florence Nightingale added. 'But in the place outside time, we have the ability to manipulate the hours if necessary and have elected to let it pass while you slept. After all, what good would it have done you to arrive back in London at six o'clock in the morning with who knows what dangers waiting for you and eighteen hours to fill?'

She left the room, closing the door gently behind her. Cal and Janey sat up in their beds.

'What do you reckon they've decided?' asked Janey.

'I just hope they managed to persuade Mr Churchill it's worth rescuing Dad and Jean.'

'After what you said, they've got to. You were amazing when you talked about showing Thorne that we're not going to give up. How did you do it?'

'Do what?'

'Speak so confidently?'

'I think it's got something to do with the Pod. The more I wear it, the more I seem to know… or at least feel like I know. When I spoke, I really believed what I was saying, so it didn't matter who I was telling, not even Winston Churchill. It's weird. I'm probably not making any sense. Ignore me.'

'I think it makes sense,' said Janey. 'You seem older now than when all this started, more sure of things. Maybe the Pod is making you stronger, teaching you in some way.'

Cal blushed and looked away. He took a long sip of tea before speaking.

'Are you ready to go?' he asked.

'Yeah, although I could use a bath,' said Janey.

'Me too,' he said, smiling grimly. 'But there's no time.'

They made the beds and were about to leave the

room when Cal turned to his friend. He looked at the floorboards, avoiding eye contact.

'Janey, I just wanted to say that… you know… whatever happens out there tonight, it's… you know, I… I mean…'

'Listen, Cal, if you're trying to say thanks, forget about it. This is what friends are for, right? Besides, if I was bored, I'd have dropped out ages ago. Now come on, we're wasting time.'

Cal smiled and opened the door. Janey followed him, shaking her head.

Crisp evening darkness had arrived, and gas lamps were flickering, creating a subtle light in which cigar and pipe smoke slowly danced. From outside the building, there was no sound.

The four legendary figures were seated in front of the hearth as if no time had passed since the children had gone to sleep. Charles Dickens smiled at them from a battered armchair and Winston Churchill sat hunched and brooding, a fat cigar in his mouth and a glass of whisky in his hand. Florence Nightingale was perched straight-backed on the edge of her seat, her hands still clasped in her lap, and Sherlock Holmes was sitting cross-legged on the floor with a large pipe in his mouth. His eyes were still shut.

'Come, children, and stand by the fire,' said Miss Nightingale.

They did so, glad for its warmth.

'Well, my brave young adventurers,' said Charles Dickens. 'We have been deep in discussion and are ready to offer our advice. The question is, are you ready to hear it?'

'Yes,' Cal and Janey replied together.

'Very well,' said Dickens, sitting back in his chair. 'It is clear we are entering a new era of peril, as the Mist once again grows strong. This has given us two distinct problems. Firstly, we are looking at perhaps many years of disruption to the human world. When the Mist gathers, chaos has been known to reign. We are standing on a precipice of unknown depths and must guard ourselves against it. Two of the Nephilim, namely Thorne and Cain, have made their presence known and it is likely that others around the globe will be doing the same.'

Each Blue Plaque member nodded and Dickens continued.

'The second issue is that of the immediate fate of the Aldhelm and the Baudouin. Thorne's demand to exchange them for the Pods is untenable and none here will condone such action.'

Cal's heart tumbled into his ribcage.

'But, we are in agreement that to abandon these two loyal servants to such a dreadful fate would be indefensible and, to use your own words, Master Wainwright, none of us wishes to roll over and do what they want.'

Cal felt a surge of hope. 'You mean we can help Dad?'

'Don't interrupt your elders, boy,' growled Mr Churchill.

'Sorry.'

'It's all right, Winston,' said Mr Dickens. 'One can understand his enthusiasm.'

He turned to Cal. 'We will countenance an attempt to rescue the Pod Guardians but are ourselves unable to intervene beyond the place outside time. You must understand that any action taken will be determined by you alone. It is your decision, Aldhelm.'

'You mean we'd have to rescue them without your help?' asked Janey.

'Correct,' replied Dickens.

'But how are we gonna do that on our own?' argued Janey. 'There are thousands of Severals, and although I'm not scared of Thorne, he's gonna be tricky to handle. We're only kids.'

'Janey, wait,' said Cal. He turned to Mr Dickens. 'There's got to be something you can tell us that will help, something we can use. We can't beat Thorne alone, you know that.'

Charles Dickens nodded.

'There is a resource available that could aid you in your struggle. It is not without its own dangers, and no Aldhelm before you has ever succeeded in using it. But should you harness the power, you may gain significant advantage.'

'What is it?' asked Cal, his heart beginning to thud.

'The Lords of the Chattan,' said Mr Dickens, leaning forward.

'The what?' asked Janey.

'Although the Nephilim are powerful, there is a chance the Lords of the Chattan would be a match for them. You must decide whether you are willing to call them to battle.'

'But Twilight told us she was no match for a Nephilim,' said Cal, confused. 'I don't see how any Chattan can help us. How many of these lords are there?'

'There are four,' said Sherlock Holmes, his eyes still shut. 'And they are far from ordinary Chattan. It is true that in great numbers, Chattan can overwhelm a single Nephilim, although you would need a thousand at least to stand a chance of it. But the Chattan Lords have a power to rival the Nephilim. The very sight of them might just be enough to send Thorne and his army back into the dank corners from which they have emerged. Perhaps for good.'

'Where can we find these cats?' asked Janey.

Mr Holmes' eyes flicked open and he regarded her coldly.

'Do not speak of them as cats,' he snapped. 'It is the Landseer Lions you must raise.'

'Landsee-what?' said Janey, confused. 'I don't get it.'

'Foolish girl,' scolded Holmes. 'What do they teach you in school these days? It is the Landseer Lions of Trafalgar Square you must awaken, and quickly.'

'The ones that all the tourists sit on?' asked Cal. Sherlock Holmes smiled and nodded. 'But how can we wake them? They're statues.'

Holmes sighed. It was Miss Nightingale who spoke next.

'The Chattan Lords were positioned in Trafalgar Square in 1867. The Aldhelm at the time set protection on them in accordance with their wishes, disguising them as statues. They have not been woken since that day and should only be summoned when most needed. We here feel that now is such a time.'

'What do I have to do?' said Cal.

'Have patience, Master Wainwright. You see, not every Aldhelm is strong enough to raise them. Your own grandmother tried it before, most recently during the last world war. Despite her outstanding reputation, she failed.'

Winston Churchill cleared his throat.

'A fine woman, your grandmother, and a brilliant Aldhelm,' he growled. 'Few have dealt with evil on such a scale. If it wasn't for her, God knows what could have happened.'

'Be that as it may, Winston,' retorted Florence Nightingale. 'If she'd managed to rouse the Chattan Lords, perhaps things could have been brought to a more speedy conclusion.'

'If my grandmother couldn't wake them, how can I? I'm not even a proper Aldhelm,' interrupted Cal.

'Consider what has happened to you, Master Wainwright,' said Charles Dickens. 'All the decisions you have made that have brought you here, to us. You have done this through instinct, without formal training of any kind. That is a rare quality indeed, perhaps the very evidence of your potential. Someday, someone has to be strong enough. Perhaps that someone is you. We must hope and believe that it is.'

'But I couldn't have done it without Janey, or Twilight,' Cal replied.

Janey beamed at him.

'A good Aldhelm chooses their allies carefully,' said Sherlock Holmes.

'How do I wake them?' Cal asked.

'You must stand before them and speak of your need,' answered Florence Nightingale. 'Be strong of heart and do not doubt your own conviction, not for a second. If you are the one destined to release them, they will come.'

'There's no guarantee though?' asked Janey.

'They cannot be tamed and will only take instruction from the one who earns their trust and respect. Only the one who is strong enough will stand a chance.'

A hush descended, broken only by the crackling fire. A chime from the clock on the mantel shelf caused Cal to look up.

'It is quarter to nine in the world governed by time,' said Mr Dickens. 'You must get ready to leave.'

'Are you willing to try, Master Wainwright?' asked Florence Nightingale.

All eyes in the room rested on him.

Cal shrugged. 'What have I got to lose?'

Charles Dickens nodded his approval.

'Then gather your things.'

Cal and Janey stood up and went through to the bedroom, closing the door behind them.

'What do you reckon?' asked Janey.

'I have to try,' said Cal, pulling on his coat.

The thought of giant lions waking after decades, and listening to him ask for help, made him feel sick. The difference between success and failure meant life or death to Jeb and Jean Legard, perhaps even to the world.

He strapped the rucksack on in silence.

'I wish Twilight was here,' he said. 'She might be able to help persuade the lions to help.'

TWENTY-NINE

Hear Me And Answer

The Blue Plaque members stood, ready to say their farewells. Apart from Mr Dickens.

'I shall accompany you as close to Trafalgar Square as possible,' he said.

Sherlock Holmes gave them a cursory nod before whirling away to stand at the window. Winston Churchill leaned on his stick and shook their hands solemnly. Florence Nightingale took their hands in both of hers, wishing them "Godspeed".

'Thank you for your advice, and for a place to rest,' said Cal.

Before leaving the room, Janey looked at Sherlock Holmes.

'How did you know those things about me?' she asked.

The detective didn't turn from the window.

'You have a number of badges pinned on your coat. Amongst them is one with a picture of piano keys. I deduce that a proud teacher or parent gave it to you after an exam. However, you wear it in a less prominent area than your other badges. Therefore, it seems of less importance, a past glory. The grazes on your knees are evidence of a fondness for climbing and the markings are from the bark of trees, oak to be precise. From that, it would be natural to assume a future career such as mountain climbing would be a dream.'

'What about the bike?' Janey asked.

This time, Sherlock Holmes turned to her.

'Simple. Every active twelve-year-old would relish a new bicycle,' he said.

Janey smiled before turning to the door. The three great figures watched them leave, saying nothing more.

*

Waiting for them in the street was an old-fashioned horse-drawn carriage. It was black, with two large wheels. Lamps containing candles sat on either side of its roof and glass windows were framed in each side panel. The horse stood patiently, head alert, its coat glimmering in the half-light. There was no driver. It looked strange, waiting against the backdrop of modern-day Baker Street that was not Baker Street at all, with its electric streetlamps, yellow lines and parked cars.

'This should make things a little more comfortable,' said Mr Dickens.

He crossed the pavement and opened the carriage's wooden doors. Cal and Janey stepped up inside and made themselves comfortable on the plush leather seat. Mr Dickens climbed in last and sat between them, pulling the wooden doors closed. They only came halfway up the front of the carriage, so that passengers were able to lean forward and look out.

'A Hansom cab is the only way to travel in London,' sighed the novelist. 'Pall Mall, please!'

The horse pulled away, the rhythmic clang of hooves and grind of wheels permeating the void.

Of all his journeys so far, Cal found this one the strangest. It was something he could barely have imagined just a few days before. He shook his head in wonder at the bizarre world in which he was now so deeply involved.

They sat in silence as the carriage crossed empty junctions, turning into Wigmore Street and then right into St James's Street. To Cal, the place outside time looked exactly like London in all but one way.

'It's so quiet,' whispered Janey, summing up his thoughts. 'There's no car fumes or sirens or people beeping their horns, nothing at all. It's amazing.'

'Sometimes we of the Blue Plaques yearn for the hustle and bustle of real London. It is but a distant memory to us now,' said Dickens. 'But there is something to be said for the peace and quiet outside time. It makes for excellent debate, without distraction.'

'Has London changed much since you… well, you know…?' said Janey.

The novelist laughed ruefully. 'Since I died, you mean? It is almost unrecognisable. In both good ways, and bad,' he said.

They travelled eastwards, behind Mayfair, before turning south into New Bond Street, its grand parade of shops empty, resembling a deserted theatre set. Cal watched for any sign of the Severals, but there were none. By the time they'd turned into Pall Mall, their ears had grown used to the skitter and rumble of wheels.

'Well, children, this is where I alight,' said Dickens as the horse slowed to a halt. 'You must go on from here alone.'

He opened the doors and stepped down onto the pavement.

'Aren't you taking the carriage back to Baker Street?' asked Cal.

'No, it will take you a little further on, to Trafalgar Square. I am going back into the Plaque Network through Number 79.'

He pointed with his cane and Cal looked up to a blue plaque on the wall of a grand building:

In a house on this site lived Nell Gwynne from 1671-1687

'Who's Nell Gwynne?' asked Janey. 'I've never heard of her.'

'Ah well, Miss Janey, may I suggest, with respect,

that when all this is done, you take the opportunity to look her up. It is a most intriguing story and she a most intriguing woman,' said Mr Dickens with a wry smile. 'And now, my brave adventurers, I wish you the very best of luck, though I trust you will not need it.' He held his hand out to them and they shook it in turn. 'Have faith, and things will turn out for the best. You have the Pods and you have each other.'

He raised a hand in farewell and Cal caught a last glimpse of the sparkle in his eyes before the horse pulled away and he was gone. Almost immediately, Cal found himself missing the great novelist. Dickens had helped to steady his nerves. Despite Janey's presence, he suddenly felt very alone.

As they entered Trafalgar Square, the horse came to a stop.

Nelson's Column towered over them. At its base lay the four lion statues, their great heads staring proudly north, south, east and west. The sky above was cloudless, the stars glimmering crisply.

The children stepped down from the carriage and Janey patted the horse's neck in thanks before it started walking once more, heading slowly across the deserted square and out of sight.

Cal swallowed as he approached the statues. They were massive, the size of small lorries. Their faces were both proud and fierce, with teeth like daggers. Neither child spoke until, eventually, Cal shook himself out of his trance.

'I guess I should get on with it,' he said.

'Yeah,' said Janey, her head tipped back as she gazed up at the nearest lion. 'You know, it's funny,' she continued, 'I can remember sitting on the back of one of these when I was really young, with Mum and Dad. Who'd have thought that one day a mate of mine would be trying to wake them up so they can help us fight a battle?'

Cal hardly heard her as he drew out the Pod, feeling its warmth beneath his jumper. Podlight spilled out, spreading across the statues.

'You'd better stand back a bit,' said Cal. 'I don't want you to get hurt.'

'Come off it. If these things are vicious, a few metres won't make much difference!'

Cal couldn't help smiling. He linked his arm with hers.

He took a deep breath and raised the Pod towards the lion closest to him. Unsure what to say, he paused, knowing it could make the difference between the Lords of the Chattan agreeing to help or not. But when he began speaking, words flowed out of him from somewhere deep within; a secret part of himself that, until now, he didn't know existed.

'Lords of the Chattan, I stand before you as temporary Pod Guardian of England. My father, the real Aldhelm, has become aware of a rising of the Mist, the like of which has not been seen for decades. But he and the Baudouin of Paris have been captured by a Nephilim called Thorne. He's raised an army of Severals against us and demanded that the Pods of England and France are handed to him in exchange for the lives of their Guardians.'

Cal's mouth was so dry he was finding it difficult to speak. He took a breath before continuing.

'I have consulted the brethren of the Blue Plaques, who advise that we may have a chance to defeat the Nephilim and release the Pod Guardians. But only with your help. Not only would this be a show of defiance to the agents of the Mist, but it may also end their current assault. I beg you to hear me and answer my call.'

He finished, his chest heaving. Janey stared at him, her jaw wide open.

'How was that?' he asked.

'Bloody awesome!'

'Thanks,' he replied, embarrassed.

After a moment, his initial elation faded. The Podlight had dimmed. Cal lowered his arm and Janey stamped her feet against the cold. Nothing stirred in Trafalgar Square. A layer of mist was rising, diluting any light from the moon and stars. It thickened steadily into a grey veil around them, coating them with a sheen of moisture.

'Nothing's happening, Cal, except this mist is getting thicker. What are we gonna do?' said Janey. Her nose and cheeks were blushed with the cold.

Cal looked at the lion, its head staring defiantly, unhearing or uncaring. He took a step forward, paused and then hauled himself up onto the concrete plinth so that he was level with the huge sculpture. He gazed up at its smooth surface and suddenly felt foolish. The Blue Plaque Network had been kidding themselves that he could rouse these magnificent statues into life. It was as he'd thought; he was just a kid, a kid way out of his depth.

He looked back at the lion and hesitated before reaching towards it. As his fingers brushed the metal surface, he immediately withdrew them, as though he'd received an electric shock.

'What's wrong?' cried Janey.

'It's warm,' he said, staring at the statue. 'The metal's warm.'

Sure enough, faint wisps of steam were rising from its surface. He stepped back as the lion's metal flank rose up slowly then fell gently again. It paused and then swelled again before falling. Rising and falling, rising and falling. The statue was breathing. Powerful muscles tensed in the lion's neck and there was a metallic, grating sound as the huge head began to turn.

Cal leapt down from the ledge. Grabbing Janey's hand, they backed away slowly.

Thick banks of steam were rising from all four lions. Even from a distance, Cal could see the great beasts' sides swelling as they took gulps of air, tasting life for the first time in over a hundred and forty years. One tossed its shaggy head, another opened and closed its jaws with dull metallic clangs, letting its tongue loll in and out. The dark bronze of the statues shimmered and brightened in intensity, its colour and texture slowly altering. The lion that Cal had touched shook his mane and water flew across the square, sounding like tropical rain on the paving slabs. With a low groan, it flexed its claws, scratching at the concrete plinth before slowly, very slowly, pushing itself up onto its feet. Its legs shook as un-worked muscles strained across its vast body. The bronze continued to transform and soon the metal had been replaced by thick golden fur. With a final effort, the great beast heaved itself up. It arched its back and yawned before gazing around Trafalgar Square through sunlight-yellow eyes.

'You did it, Cal. You really did it,' Janey whispered.

The other lions followed the first, pushing themselves up on unsteady legs, standing like newborn calves, flexing joints and stretching their bodies, testing themselves. They dipped their heads to the concrete fountains and lapped at the water, quenching an ancient thirst. Then they began to move about, their strength steadily returning. Soon they were jogging up and down, working their muscles. Moments later, they were running and leaping around the square like kittens, jumping at one another playfully, sending miniature earthquakes across the surface of the concrete, spilling water from the fountain pools.

Cal and Janey laughed as the lions played, and their eyes filled with tears at the beauty of it.

'They're magnificent,' said Janey, her voice shaking.

'I'm going to talk to them,' said Cal.

'Are you sure?'

'I have to.'

'Well, I've come this far. I'm not letting you go alone.'

'Stay close then, and no sudden moves. I'll show them the Pod, maybe that'll help.'

As they moved, one of the lions swung its head towards them. It growled and jogged forward, stopping a short distance away. Its bittersweet breath enveloped the children. Behind, the other lions had stopped playing and were padding across the square to stand next to one another in a row, bristling with power. Cal could barely prevent himself from running in the opposite direction.

'Maybe this was a mistake,' squeaked Janey.

'Keep going,' Cal answered.

They advanced a few more steps before stopping. The lions watched intently as banks of steam left their bodies in swirling clouds. Cal inhaled, counted to ten, and then slowly lifted the Pod from around his neck, holding it in front of him. Blue light poured from it at his touch, easing into the darkness. The lions didn't flinch at its glare.

'Lords of the Chattan!' called Cal. 'As time grows short, I ask again, will you join us in battle?'

The lions stared back, with inscrutable expressions. Then from somewhere distant, a deep rumbling resonated through the ground, growing more pronounced until it vibrated up through the children's legs and caused their teeth to chatter.

'They're purring, Janey,' he cried. 'They're purring!'

Close up, their purrs were deafening, and Cal was overwhelmed with a sense of colossal power. A flick of their giant paws and the children would be crushed instantly. The Chattan Lords circled the children before one of them dropped down on its belly and turned its yellow eyes on them.

'What does it want?' whispered Janey, gripping Cal's arm.

'I think it wants us to get on its back. Come on, I'll help you,' he said.

Janey put a foot in his hands and pushed herself onto the lion's back, grasping its golden mane. Cal scrambled up behind her. No sooner were they comfortable than the lion stood.

'To Parliament Hill,' cried Cal.

With an almighty roar, the lions started jogging along the road.

'Hang on!' Cal added, wrapping his arms around Janey's waist.

The sound of the lions' paws boomed like thunder as they accelerated into a run, and soon it resembled a great storm raging throughout the city streets.

They headed up Charing Cross Road, increasing their pace. Wind flowed through the children's hair and tears ran from their eyes. Cal glanced at a clock hanging from the face of a building and saw that it was almost quarter to midnight. He strengthened his grip.

With little more than fifteen minutes until they were due to meet the Nephilim, they sped north as lengthening fingers of mist closed about them.

THIRTY

Close At Hand

Marylebone Road was deserted as they crossed towards Camden. Buildings whizzed by in a blur, and glass windows in shopfronts shook as they passed by. Where the streets were too narrow for them to run side by side, the Chattan Lords ran in single file, leaping over parked cars with the sheer joy of their momentum. With each huge stride, the mist continued to thicken, so that the streetlamps soon shone with silvery halos in the soupy gloom.

Cal glimpsed Camden tube station and felt the muscles of the lion tense as the railway bridge spanning the high street approached. Realising what was about to happen, he closed his eyes as the lions sprang, leaving the tarmac behind. He held his breath as they soared over the bridge, the silhouettes of a thousand chimney pots across London's skyline rising above the mist alongside them. He braced himself for the coming impact, but the lion landed so softly it was as if they had dropped onto a street of marshmallow.

Onward they ran, north through Chalk Farm into Belsize Park. Entering Hampstead, the thunderstorm of thudding paws subsided as the lions slowed.

They turned into Downshire Hill, where Victorian streetlamps glowed in the mist, conjuring images of the thick smog of old London. Cal looked at the church clock. It was five to midnight. The journey from Trafalgar Square had taken just ten minutes.

Halfway along the street, Cal spotted a blue plaque on the front of a tall terraced house. He could just make out the letters and numbers, *Lee Miller, 1907-1977*, in white letters.

'Wait!' he called out. 'We need to get back to real time.'

The lions stopped abruptly. Cal knew the Podlight would be blazing beneath his jacket. He drew it out, and blue light surged until they were completely suspended in its glare. A beam connected Pod and plaque before flicking off abruptly, leaving them on the pavement once more. The drone of London hovered in the air.

'Okay, let's go,' Cal said.

The length of the lions' strides meant that, even at walking pace, they arrived at the heath in seconds. They crossed the grass, following a pathway between two ponds. It swept up and to the right, lined by trees and more Victorian streetlamps. Cal felt the Pod grow icy against his skin.

'Stop,' he called in a loud whisper.

The lions pulled up and Cal and Janey swung down to stand on the path.

'Wait here,' he commanded.

Eight eyes watched as he led Janey a little further up the path.

'I need to go on alone, Janey.'

'No way, Cal, I've come this far…'

'I *have* to go on alone. You need to wait here with the lions and come when you hear my signal.'

'But it's gonna be dangerous up there. Why don't we go together, you, me and the lions?'

'Because if Thorne sees we're going to resist him, I don't know what he'll do to Dad and Jean. We need to surprise him at just the right time.' Cal could see doubt clouding Janey's face. 'Look, I wouldn't ask this if it wasn't important. You think I want to go up there on my own?'

'No.'

'Well, there you go. You need to be ready when I call, okay?'

Janey hesitated, thinking it over and then nodded. 'Okay, deal.'

'Great,' said Cal. 'I've only got a minute, so I have to go.'

They walked back to where the lions were standing, tense and alert.

'Lords of the Chattan,' he said solemnly. 'I'll summon you when I need you. Don't show yourselves until then. Watch for the Aldhelm and the Baudouin, they mustn't be harmed.'

The lions didn't move, but somehow Cal knew they had understood. He turned and walked up the path. Looking back, he saw Janey with her hand resting on the mane of the lion that had carried them.

'Be careful,' she called.

Cal tried to smile and then turned away, following the path around the corner and out of sight.

As he approached Parliament Hill, the trees opened up, falling away on either side. The streetlamps went no further, and mist skulked thickly over the grass, giving the impression that he was walking on a cloud.

Cal felt the unmistakable presence of Severals and could hear their excited sniffing. The Pod had grown so cold it felt as though it was burning. But he knew it was trying to help; warning him, protecting him. His legs were becoming impossibly heavy, and when at last the path levelled out, he stopped and took a deep breath before lifting his head.

Even after everything he'd seen in the last week, the sight that met Cal's eyes filled him with terror. He took a backward step.

Surrounding him as far as the eye could see were the Severals. Quivering with excitement, they hung from the branches of trees and hovered in the sky above. Their bodies lined Parliament Hill in all directions. Where the heath ended and houses began, they hung from window ledges and perched on chimney pots, their blind eyes turned towards him. The air reverberated with snorts and heaved with their throbbing. The view of London, normally such a wide vista from here, was completely obscured. Only shifting darkness could be seen, blotting out the very stars in the sky. Cal felt loathing flow through him. He yearned for the Pod's comforting light but he left it concealed, wanting to ensure the moment to reveal it was right. The temptation to call for the lions was strong, but Cal knew he had to wait; do it too early and it could mean certain death for Jeb and Legard.

The wheezing hiss of Thorne's laughter slithered across the hilltop. Goosebumps ran over Cal's body as he tried to work out which direction it was coming from. The Severals were packed so tightly together that the effect was confusing. The laughter circled him before dying away.

'And so he has come!' came Thorne's grating whisper.

The Severals throbbed eagerly as they sensed the Nephilim's approach.

*

Janey watched Cal move out of sight and stood quietly, waiting. She was still hurt that he had not wanted her to go with him and was impatient to know what was going on. She thought quickly, gathering the bravery to speak.

'Wait here, I'm just going to check on something up ahead,' she said to the lions, with as much authority as she could muster.

As an afterthought, she pulled out Legard's Pod, hoping it would add some gravitas to her words. The lions watched, and a low rumble came from the chest of the one closest to her.

'Don't worry, I'll be two minutes,' she said, moving away up the path.

The lions watched her until she turned the corner. Seeing that they had obeyed her, she continued forward, crouching low and keeping close to the bushes. The mist made it difficult to see. Janey stopped, uncertain, wondering if she should turn back. But curiosity got the better of her. Why should she wait with them anyway? Surely they would know what to do.

She contented herself with this thought and was about to set off again when a shadow moved somewhere in the trees to her right. Janey crouched low, holding her breath. As she turned back towards the lions, a hand was clamped roughly over her mouth before she could so much as whimper. A silhouette moved out of the trees and a face loomed into view.

THIRTY-ONE

Deliverance

———————

'At least you arrived on time, Wainwright,' Thorne wheezed. 'That bodes well for your father. I just hope you're able to fulfil the rest of our agreement.'

'Where are you?' Cal called out.

'First, I want evidence that you have the Pods,' replied Thorne.

'You'll see nothing until I know the Guardians are safe,' Cal called. He wasn't sure how far he could push the Nephilim, but knew that showing his hand too soon would be dangerous.

'You are in no position to bargain,' snapped Thorne.

'I've got what you want. You can't take them by force, so if you want the Pods you have to listen.'

The Nephilim hissed a string of words in some strange tongue.

'You are coming of age, Wainwright, but your impudence may be your undoing. Do not cross me.'

Cal said nothing. His heart was hurling itself against his ribs and his brow was slick with sweat.

'Very well,' barked Thorne.

Sensing movement to his right, Cal turned to see Severals peeling back from the path, creating a tunnel around it. A figure stood at the opposite end. An orange glow from the tip of a cigarette glimmered in the darkness.

'Are you coming then?' Thorne wheezed.

Cal moved cautiously through the Severals, so that just a few centimetres prevented them from touching him. Guarding against the anger he could feel growing within him, he stopped a few feet short of Thorne. The Nephilim smirked at him.

'Closer,' he goaded.

Cal hesitated and then took a step forward. This was as close as he had ever been to Thorne and he wrinkled his nose at the smell that hung about the Nephilim, an odour that made him think of rotting meat. Thorne took a drag on his cigarette and blew the smoke in Cal's face.

'Where are they?' asked Cal, waving it away.

Thorne stood aside and chuckled, a sound like shovels scraping on gravel.

Just a few paces behind him, Jeb and Legard knelt on the path, facing the ground. Severals held them in position and yanked their heads back roughly. They stared at him without recognition, lifeless and exhausted, their faces pale. Dark rings circled their eyes.

'What's wrong with them?'

Thorne sneered and took another drag on his cigarette before answering.

'Let's just say they've spent a little too much time in the company of Severals than is healthy. The effects may wear off quite quickly once they're released, although I'm not so sure about the Baudouin, he's old and weak. Besides, his Nephilim has spent time alone with him, and Cain's not quite as civilised as myself.'

The click of metal-heeled shoes on the path behind him caused Cal to turn around. A young man emerged through the Severals. He was sharply dressed in a grey suit and wore a trilby hat. From beneath it, long dark hair ran down his back. Small round sunglasses perched on rigid cheekbones and he carried a cane in his hand, his talons curled around the handle.

Cain walked to Legard and stood over him, running his talons through the Frenchman's hair before whispering something into his ear. Tears welled in the old man's eyes and ran down his face, splashing onto the path. Cain smiled at Cal and lifted his hat in mock greeting, smiling coldly before Thorne turned back, blocking his view.

'Now, Wainwright,' he said. 'Give me the Pods and spare your father and the old man further torment.'

Part of Cal longed to hand over the Pods; the other wanted to resist. He had left Legard's with Janey, knowing that the temptation to surrender them might be too great.

Thorne watched him, a look of greed on his face. Cal reached inside his coat to where the Pod hung like a shard of ice. He took a deep breath before lifting it high above his head.

'Lords of the Chattan, I summon you now!' he cried. 'Heed the call of the Aldhelm and fight with me!'

Thorne's face flashed surprise, quickly turning to rage. The Pod burned more brightly than Cal had seen before and a series of blue rays shot from it in bursts of energy, cutting deep into the Severals, scattering them and evaporating any it touched. The power of it sent Cal flying backwards through the air to land, dazed, on the grass. He struggled to his knees, realising he had been thrown some twenty feet from the path.

While the bursts of light from the Pod continued to tear into the Severals, they made no impact on the Nephilim, bouncing off them harmlessly. Thorne was striding across the heath towards Cal, with Cain alongside. Their expressions exuded such raw anger that Cal could hardly look as they approached. He tried to scramble up but slipped as they bore down on him. He caught a scent of rotting flesh as they ripped the sunglasses from their faces, revealing white, soulless eyes like polished marble beneath. Cal threw his hand across his face and waited.

A sudden series of screeches sounded from lower down the hill and he peered through his fingers to see a small army of bodies hurtle out of the mist. It was the Chattan, hundreds of them. They tore through the Severals, heading for the Nephilim. Thorne and Cain wheeled around to meet them, braced and ready, their teeth bared.

Cal scrabbled to his feet and turned away, taking the opportunity to make for the spot where he had last seen Jeb and Legard. The Pod unleashed a series of blinding flashes that scythed through any Severals in its path, attempting to carve an opening through them. He had begun to make progress when something jumped up at him from the darkness, landing on his shoulder.

'Twilight!' he cried out.

'Are you all right, Cal?' she asked, nuzzling him.

'Yeah, I think so.'

'Where's Jeb?'

'Over there by the path, I'm trying to get to him.'

A little way to their left, Thorne and Cain stood back-to-back, slashing wildly, scything down cat after cat with ease. But the Chattan kept coming, pinning them in place.

'I must go to their aid, Cal,' said Twilight. 'We'll hold them as long as we can. Find your father.'

And then she sprang away to join the others. The Chattan tore and bit with renewed fury as hundreds of Severals flocked to the aid of the Nephilim. There wasn't much time.

Cal stumbled onward as bolts of Podlight jetted in all directions, destroying any Severals that came too near. But for each one that was destroyed, another ten seemed to fill its place. Visibility was near impossible and he struggled slowly through the mayhem. He hadn't got far when something sharp raked across his cheek, sending him sprawling to the ground. Flipping himself over, he saw Thorne standing above him, his chest heaving.

'You fool. Did you really think that the Pod and a few cats could defeat two Nephilim and the largest army of Severals ever assembled?' he screamed.

'Who betrayed us?' Cal shouted back. 'What's Gretchley's name now?'

Thorne struck him across the face, slamming his head against the ground. Cal tasted blood.

'I warned you not to anger me.'

The Nephilim's face was distorted with fury and he raised his talons, ready to swipe. But before he could do so, a booming roar blasted across the heath, scattering the Severals like dead leaves in a hurricane.

Thorne's eyes widened.

'You raised them?' he said. 'How could you have known?'

'Maybe I'm stronger than you think,' answered Cal.

Thorne moved closer, until their faces almost touched.

'You may be strong, Wainwright, stronger even than your grandmother, but this is just the beginning. I will remember your betrayal, and I promise that before you die, you will have cause to fear me. You will regret the very day you were born.'

With that, Thorne hurled him to the ground and turned away. Cain loomed silently out of the mist and together they waited.

Cal hauled himself up. Severals fled as the lions appeared on the hilltop, smashing into them like skittles, crushing and breaking them without mercy, each fall of their giant paws shaking the earth underfoot. They cleared a wide path towards the Nephilim, who had crouched, ready to defend themselves.

As Cal watched, Thorne and Cain's human forms began to change; twisting into other beastlike bodies, strange hybrids somewhere between savage dogs and wild boars. Their matted fur writhed with insects and weeping wounds opened, dripping steaming pus onto the ground. Muscles strained beneath their skin and their necks pulsed thickly. Dark saliva drooled from their mouths, collecting in puddles at their feet.

As two of the lions broke towards them, the Nephilim leapt forward, snarling. Although half the size of the Chattan Lords, they fought viciously, scratching with their filthy talons at golden fur, opening the flesh in jagged strips. While the lions had the advantage of size and strength, the Nephilim were quick, and their bodies changed rapidly, never settling for too long. One minute they became men again, and then they were vultures, pecking at the eyes of their foe, and next they were pig-dog creatures once more. The fight was fierce and so fast that Cal could barely follow it.

'Cal! Cal! Over here!' came a voice across the battlefield.

Cal turned to where a small band of people were making their way through the space the lions had cleared. Janey was amongst them waving at him and he ran towards her, bolts of Podlight still picking off any Severals that attempted an approach. As he got closer, the blue light pierced the mist, revealing Janey's companions.

''Ello, Cal!' said a deep voice.

Baron sprang into view, his sword flashing in his hand as he and his crew slashed and hacked their way towards him.

'How did you get here?' exclaimed Cal. 'I thought...'

'Listen, boy,' Baron said with a grunt as he neatly dispatched another Several. 'You don't get to my age and not learn 'ow to look after yerself. Nah what I mean?'

Cal felt almost relieved to see the old cut-throat. He let the protection of the Podlight wash over the pirates, enabling them to catch their breath.

Cal glanced back to the Nephilim, and he saw that now only one of them fought on, twisting and leaping to avoid the blows of the Chattan Lords. He scoured the area but couldn't see the other.

An ugly croak from above caused him to look up to where a gigantic vulture was soaring in the night sky, silhouetted against the stars. Cal watched as it circled Parliament Hill, taking in the scene below.

'Thorne,' he muttered under his breath.

The transformed Nephilim fixed its gaze on him before barking out another hideous cry. It banked north, heading away from the city. Cal watched until he could see it no longer, and then turned back to the pirates.

'I've got to find Dad,' he said. 'Can you help me?'

Baron gave an elaborate bow. 'We are at your service, young man.'

'This way.'

The pirates moved as one unit, with Cal and Janey at their centre. The Podlight surrounded them, keeping any remaining Severals at a safe distance.

As they neared the path, Cal could see Legard kneeling at its edge. He was cradling Jeb's head in his lap.

'Jean!' cried Cal.

The Baudouin glanced up briefly, but his eyes were vacant, his snowy hair lank and greasy. Stubble lined his chin. He looked back down at Jeb, his shoulders slumped.

'Hurry!' urged Cal.

They were almost there when Cain leapt from the darkness, landing lightly at Legard's side. Battered and bleeding, somehow he'd evaded the lions. Legard didn't attempt to struggle as the Nephilim wrenched him by the hair, speaking quietly into his ear.

'No,' cried Cal, running forward. 'Stop him.'

Cain threw Legard to the floor. He ran at Cal, talons raised and teeth bared. His eyes were full of cruelty, and dark smudges of blood were smeared across his face like war paint. But before he could make contact, Baron jumped between them, swinging his sword at the Nephilim's head. Cain raised his hands and crossed them at the wrists, using his talons to parry the blow. Thrown off balance, the river pirate let his guard down and the Nephilim moved quickly, raking his talons across Baron's chest with a force that hurled him to the ground. Baron twisted and rolled, eventually lying still.

Cain licked his lips and looked at Cal, pointing.

'You!' he rasped. His face was twisted, and his overcoat billowed out behind him.

He was within two strides of Cal when the blow struck him. In one fearsome swipe, Cain's body snapped like a twig and was thrown across the battlefield, landing awkwardly. He shuddered and jerked where he lay. Emerging from the fog, the lion that had struck the deadly blow unleashed a thundering roar. It slammed its paw down on the Nephilim's body with a sickening crunch and the ground lurched. And then it was gone, chasing and harrying through the mist.

Cain did not move again.

The remaining Severals seethed with panic, looking to escape any way they could. The Chattan Lords continued their pursuit, sweeping across Parliament Hill until it was clear of the throbbing shadows, allowing moonlight to cast its silvery sheen over Hampstead Heath.

Cal ran to Jeb and gently turned him onto his back. Baron limped out of the gloom, his wounds forgotten, and knelt at the Aldhelm's side. He put an ear to his chest and listened before putting a hand on Cal's shoulder.

'It's okay, boy, yer dad's breathing,' he said, wincing and holding a hand to his side.

Cal lifted the Pod from around his neck and placed it into Jeb's hands, closing them around it. Immediately, blue light broke through the gaps in his fingers. Jeb's eyelids fluttered as colour began to return to his cheeks and he looked about him before focusing on Cal. He frowned.

'Cal?' he asked, confused for a moment. And then his fingers tightened around the Pod. 'Cal,' he repeated. 'My Cal.'

'Shhh, Dad,' said Cal, stroking Jeb's hair. 'It's okay. You're going to be okay, but you need to rest.'

'Jean?'

'I'll check on him, Dad. Just rest now.'

Jeb smiled and closed his eyes. At a nod from Baron, one of his crew placed a cloak over the Aldhelm to keep him warm.

Cal found Janey kneeling at Jean Legard's side, holding one of the old man's hands in hers. She looked up and shook her head, tears running down her face.

'He didn't make it, Cal. He's gone,' she said, breaking into sobs.

The Pod hung grey and lifeless from the Baudouin's fingers, where Janey had placed it.

'I can't tell Dad, not yet. He needs to rest,' Cal said.

Turning to the battlefield, he saw the four lions standing proud and strong. Scattered across the grass lay numerous Chattan bodies. Of the Severals, there was no sign.

Something brushed Cal's leg and he glanced down to see Twilight, a clump of fur torn from her back and a bloody paw held in front of her.

'You have done something wondrous tonight, Cal,' she purred.

He bent forward and scooped her up.

'Careful,' she winced.

'That's twice I thought I'd lost you,' said Cal, cradling her carefully.

As he spoke, the lions let out a collective roar. The sound was deafening, shaking the earth and moving clouds as it rolled down off the heath across the rooftops of London. And then they were running, loping gracefully down the hill towards the city.

'Amazing,' said Janey, joining Cal.

They watched the lions disappear between the buildings. The vibrations became faint, until they could no longer feel them at all.

'Yeah,' was all Cal could manage.

'What are we going to do about the Chattan?' asked Janey. 'There are so many dead…'

She hesitated. Confusion clouded her face and Cal followed her gaze to where Chattan bodies had littered the heath. The grass was now clear of them.

'You needn't worry about that,' said Twilight. 'The heath is protected ground once more. Even though that protection has weakened, anything killed here in the name of the Pod needs no burial. They remain part of it forever.'

Cal turned and saw that Jean Legard's body had gone too.

'What about Cain?' he asked.

The Nephilim's broken body lay in the distance. Its limbs were jutting out at strange angles.

'He can rot where he lies,' spat Twilight.

'Leave that to us,' said Baron, limping across to join them. 'Me an' the gang'll see to it. There's plenty o' sewer rats'll make a nice meal of 'im!'

'Thorne?' asked Twilight.

'He got away,' said Cal quietly.

He pictured the ragged vulture and shivered. The Nephilim's threats surged through his head – *I will remember your betrayal, and I promise that before you die, you will have cause to fear me. You will regret the very day you were born.*

He glanced across to where Jeb now lay comfortable and safe. A mix of exhaustion and relief washed over him and he moved away from the others, cradling Twilight in his arms. The Chattan purred loudly, her eyes closed. Cal carried her towards a bench that overlooked London. He watched the stars sparkling above the sea of electric lights and sat there silently for a while.

EPILOGUE

TRAFALGAR SQUARE LONDON
SOMETIME RECENTLY

'**C**an you see her, Dad?'

'Be patient, she'll be here soon,' replied Jeb, smiling at Cal's enthusiasm.

'What does she look like?'

'I have no idea. Will you please stop fidgeting. Come and sit down.'

Cal made a face but wandered back over and sat on the concrete step next to his dad. It was a crisply cold Christmas Day morning and the sky was bright overhead. Trafalgar Square was less busy than normal, mainly determined tourists out taking photos, wrapped in coats and scarves. Apart from that, Cal and Jeb had it to themselves.

'It seems like ages ago, doesn't it? Everything that happened,' said Cal, craning his neck to look up at the bronze lion that loomed above them.

'It does,' replied Jeb, staring into the distance.

The Aldhelm had made a good recovery, but there were lines on his face and a look in his eyes that hadn't been there before. Cal knew things had happened to him that he hadn't spoken about yet; perhaps he never would. But in the days since, they had tried to get back to some sort of normal existence, even though they knew it was only temporary.

'Do you ever think about him, Dad?'

'Jean? Yes, of course. He was a good and brave man. If it wasn't for his quick thinking, Thorne's ambush might have worked. And we wouldn't be aware of Gretchley's return without him.'

Cal paused before speaking.

'When will we know who Gretchley really is and where he's hiding?'

'I've no idea. But we'll find him, whatever he calls himself now. Don't you worry about that.'

'What about Thorne and the Severals? When do you think they'll be back?'

'It could be tomorrow, or it could be in a year. Until then, we must keep our eyes and ears open as best we can, eh?'

'Yeah, I guess so.'

'Without the ravens at the Tower and the Severals free of the Labyrinth, the Podmagic has weakened. But we must hope it's enough.'

Cal had so many questions in his head but hadn't wanted to bother Jeb with them after his ordeal. The answers would become apparent sooner or later on their own.

Many times since, he even thought he may have imagined the whole thing; it all seemed so removed from reality. Part of him missed the adventures; not the bad stuff, of course. But he had desperately wanted to travel through a blue plaque again, to see Mr Dickens and the others, and there were nights when he dreamed of coming to Trafalgar Square and waking the lions. Occasionally, he thought of strange old Piccadilly, somewhere deep below.

He even wanted to see Baron and the river pirates, but they had left London shortly after the battle to undertake a long voyage. When he had raised the matter of how Twilight had persuaded Baron to help them, she had refused to tell him, saying that it was part of the agreement between the pirate and herself that it remained private. That had been the end of it.

'How's Janey doing?' Jeb asked.

'She's fine,' said Cal, smiling. 'You know Janey.'

He had only seen her once since the night on Parliament Hill. Janey had been in serious trouble after going missing, but her mum had gone easy on her seeing as it was Christmas, and she had been allowed to come to *Podwitch* for Boxing Day lunch. Cal knew she couldn't wait.

As for Dean Broad, he'd finally been seen again the day after the battle on Parliament Hill. The Chattan messengers reported that he had lost weight and was quiet, keeping himself to himself. He seemed to have no recollection of the events, but his shoulders had remained rounded and stooped, as though whatever weight had been placed there by the Nephilim had never quite gone away.

'*Monsieur Wainwright*?' said a voice in a heavy French accent, interrupting Cal's thoughts.

Jeb and Cal stood up and looked at the woman before them. She was slim and pretty with shoulder-length brown hair under a red woollen hat. Her eyes were bright blue and her cheeks a little flushed with the cold. She held out her hand in greeting and they shook it.

'*Bonjour*. I am Anne-Marie, Anne-Marie Legard,' she said with a smile.

'*Bonjour, Mademoiselle Legard*,' said Jeb, warmly. 'I'm Jeb and this is my son, Cal.'

She smiled at Cal and he saw immediately that she had her father's eyes.

'I believe you 'ave something of mine.'

'I do indeed,' replied Jeb.

He reached into his pocket and drew out the Baudouin's Pod, holding it out to her. Mademoiselle Legard hesitated before taking it, a mix of emotions crossing her face. But as her fingers made contact with it, it began to shine with intense red light. Cal felt its warmth on his face in the chilly morning air. On seeing the reaction, Jeb smiled.

'Well, you're certainly who you say you are.'

'*Merci, Monsieur*. It 'as not been easy for me these past few days. I am sorry I could not be 'ere sooner. There is much I 'ad to arrange before taking up my new responsibilities.'

'No problem,' said Jeb, 'although it's Cal you should thank. Without him, the Baudouin's Pod would have fallen into the wrong hands.'

'Don't forget Janey, Dad,' said Cal, nudging him.

'How could I forget Janey?' said Jeb, laughing.

Anne-Marie Legard turned to Cal and spoke as she put the chain over her head, slipping the Pod inside her jacket.

'*Merci beaucoup,* Cal. I understand you showed great promise. It seems the Aldhelm's Pod is in safe 'ands in future.'

Cal felt his cheeks grow hot.

'And now, I should be going,' said the new Baudouin.

'So soon?' said Jeb.

'It is Christmas Day, *non*? I don't want to interrupt your celebrations.'

'Why don't you come to *Podwitch* for dinner?' asked Cal. 'Can she, Dad?'

'I don't see why not,' said Jeb. He looked at her. 'You'd be more than welcome. We can share the food we have, and we may have a spare present or two.'

'Please say yes,' said Cal.

Miss Legard looked down at him. 'On one condition,' she said.

'What?'

'That we address each other by first names only. It's a rule my father swore by and I would like to as well.'

'Deal,' said Cal.

The three of them laughed as they made their way across the square, talking like old friends under the gaze of the Landseer Lions.

*

The man once known as Edmund Gretchley pulled the collars of his overcoat up against the cold and swore under his breath.

Next to him stood a woman with short blonde hair,

a deathly pale face, and prominent cheekbones upon which rested a pair of sunglasses. She wore a long leather jacket over a charcoal-grey skirt and high-heeled black shoes. She held her hands behind her back. A strand of dark saliva hung from the corner of her mouth.

They hovered at the edge of Trafalgar Square, staring at where Cal and the Pod Guardians had disappeared before moving away slowly. As they walked, the woman plunged her hands into her pockets, but not before her claws flashed in the sunlight.

Moments later, they were gone, and church bells began to peal over London as a flock of pigeons leapt up and rose into a sky of radiant blue.

Thanks to:

My brother, Matt, for providing the kindling for the fire, and extra fuel when needed. Tom, who first encouraged me to dust the manuscript down and make it happen. Vanessa Jones, for casting an expert eye over the revised MS, spotting all my errors and inaccuracies. My parents, Clive and Dawne, who taught me the value of stories. My wonderful wife, Laura, who believed, encouraged and bought me time and space. My son, Casper, who amazes me every day. And finally, "Bramley", who kept me company at the start of the journey but wasn't able to make it to the finish.